TIEBREAKER

TIEBREAKER

The Final Vote

BARBARA REED;
MARGIE J PITTMAN

authorHOUSE®

AuthorHouse™
1663 Liberty Drive
Bloomington, IN 47403
www.authorhouse.com
Phone: 1 (800) 839-8640

This book is a work of fiction. The characters incidents, and dialogues are the products of the
authors' imagination and are not to be construed as real. Any resemblance to actual events
or persons, living or dead is entirely coincidental. All scripture quotations are taken from
the King James Version of the Holy Bible. No part of this publication may be reproduced,
stored in a retrieval system, or transmitted in any form or by any means, electronic,
mechanical, photographic, recording, or otherwise, without prior written permission.

Published by AuthorHouse 4/25/2015

ISBN: 978-1-5049-0768-2 (sc)
ISBN: 978-1-5049-0769-9 (hc)
ISBN: 978-1-5049-0767-5 (e)

Library of Congress Control Number: 2015906085

Print information available on the last page.

Any people depicted in stock imagery provided by Thinkstock are models,
and such images are being used for illustrative purposes only.
Certain stock imagery © Thinkstock.

This book is printed on acid-free paper.

Because of the dynamic nature of the Internet, any web addresses or links contained in
this book may have changed since publication and may no longer be valid. The views
expressed in this work are solely those of the author and do not necessarily reflect the
views of the publisher, and the publisher hereby disclaims any responsibility for them.

CONTENTS

CHAPTER ONE

*

Old Stone Church

Ten year old Alex Cavender watched in horror as the huge building imploded. It was the old stone church that, according to city leaders, had stood for over one hundred years. The tall steeple, a prominent landmark in the city, now lay crushed on the ground. Alex held tightly to his mother's hand, and pretended not to see the tears slipping down her face. She was a very private person. For her to cry in public like this was a big deal to her fifth grade son. He felt like crying himself. He always loved to hear the bells on Sunday morning. They would never toll again for the people of this city. The church was completely destroyed. It was a sad day for Alex. He knew there was something going on, but he didn't know what.

His mind was full of contradictions. He felt a connection to that church, and he was sad to see it destroyed. There was a group of people called the AFA (American Freedom Association) and they had handed out pamphlets about The Law at his school. It said that The Law would free our nation of bigotry and the evils of rigid closed-mindedness. It talked a lot about political correctness and not offending others. His teacher had explained about there being no absolute right or wrong. He wasn't sure all that made sense to him. It felt like he was being pushed into things that didn't fit.

He was so troubled and so deep in thought that he forgot his mother's tears and started rattling off questions.

"What gives them the right to destroy such a beautiful old building? Why do some people hate Christians so much? Can they really put you in jail just for quoting the bible?

Jillian had been thinking through some of the same questions herself. She was proud of her son for asking such mature questions and she told him so. She didn't recognize her own voice so she quickly cleared her throat and tried to discreetly dry her eyes.

"I was just thinking to myself and wondering how we had come to this place. It seems like such a short time ago that my mother told me stories about when she was in school and they had prayer and studied the bible every day. One of the worst things to happen at school was when someone got caught chewing bubble gum in class. Since then, one at a time, Christian liberties have been taken away. They started teaching evolution as scientific fact. They took prayer out of school. They invented something called political correctness which sounded innocent enough, but turned into a mighty weapon against liberty and truth. They then used global warming and when there wasn't any warming, climate change to call anyone who disagreed with them science deniers.

There was a time not too long ago when Christians were not afraid to stand for what was right. Since then the liberal courts and the left wing have gradually eroded our freedom and vilified Christians. They even passed so called hate crime laws that made it illegal to say anything against another person's lifestyle or belief. Somehow though these laws are never applied when people speak against Christianity. They can say anything they want about Jesus or Christians, even great lies, and it is ok."

Alex was a little overwhelmed with all this information and he knew that his mother was very upset by something about this. He decided not to upset her any more. He thought he would talk to his Grandfather at Thanksgiving. He was sure he would know the

2

answers to all his question. Many times, he had heard his mom and dad discussing The Law that would soon be introduced in Washington D.C. Alex had lived there all his life. His grandfather was in politics and currently the vice president of the United States of America. Alex was always proud of his grandfather he thought that he was a wonderful politician. He had spent many years in the senate before he became vice president. The family was confident he would run for president in the next election.

CHAPTER TWO

No-Win Situation

John Paul Cavender is one of the most respected men in Washington D.C. Even as the vice president of the United States, he is very popular with both political parties. He had friends on both sides of the aisle. He has a well-deserved reputation for helping reconcile differences. He was also known for being very principled and decisive.

He was a big man in stature. He stood over six feet tall with salt and pepper hair, and warm brown eyes and he was in excellent shape. Many women found him quite attractive. Some even made a point of letting him know it. John was always polite to them and quick to tell them about his beautiful wife Rebecca. He simply wasn't interested in any other woman. Since they first met, Rebecca had always been the only woman for him.

John is a devoted family man and a politician. He loves and values both his family and his career. He always wanted to do the right thing for his fellow Americans. John hoped to run for president as soon as President William Noble's term was up. He had worked very hard toward that goal and he hadn't had a decent night's sleep in months. William's first term had passed by quickly. They had managed to do a lot of work in conjunction with their Conservative counterparts. The second term had been a nightmare. The Liberals were in power. You would have thought that was a good thing, but John Paul couldn't wait for this term to be over. He was a Liberal, but it seemed the face of the party was changing every day. He hardly recognized it anymore. There was a time when both parties could work together for the good of the country. That seemed a long time ago. These were troubled times in America. A lot of unrest among the people and the government.

John Paul sat quietly in his office evaluating his professional life. It seemed kind of dark now. The house was getting ready to introduce a new bill to the senate that could have a huge impact on John's career, and it would take a miracle for him to run for president. He feared his party was on a dangerous course. The country was divided right now and to make matters worse he knew that as soon as the senate went into session next year he would probably have to cast the tiebreaking vote. John had always voted with his party, but this would be the end of his career and he knew it. No matter how he voted, half the country would be angry with him, this was a no win situation for John. The President would expect his support for the party. What bad timing for him. The senate was divided right down the middle. John was feeling the stress of his job. He felt like a dead man walking.

Rebecca, John's wife and number one supporter had left for Texas a week ago. She had gone home to make preparations for the holidays. Becky, as he called her, loved the winter holidays. It would be a festive time with the house so full of family. Their children, grandchildren and many close friends always got together for Thanksgiving and Christmas. John would be leaving on Friday. He usually enjoyed this time of the year more than any other time. Suddenly he felt very old, and so tired he wondered how much longer he could keep up this pace. This new Congress was wearing him down. Why they had to introduce this legislation right now was beyond him.

CHAPTER THREE

Sweet Rebecca

The tall fir tree that adorned the white house was amazingly beautiful this year. Even John had a hard time remembering to call it a Holiday tree instead of a Christmas tree. John felt a catch in his throat as he stood admiring the decorations. He wondered what the next year would bring. What would become of this beautiful season? How would The Law change things?

He suddenly missed his parents. He wished they were still alive. He'd like to hear his mother sing "Silent Night" one more time. To his surprise a tear trickled down his face. John had never been a praying man, but now he wished he had listened more closely to his mother when she tried to teach him about God. She was the warmest most loving person he had ever known. She adored him and his father. John had always known that he was loved. His wife Becky was also warm and loving like his mom. John knew he was a lucky man. Suddenly he couldn't wait to go home. Just the thought of Becky made his life better. He loved to watch her joy at Christmas. She glowed through the whole season, because she was a wife, mother and grandmother, and being with her family was her favorite place to be.

Rebecca worked diligently to prepare their home for the holidays. The food was being delivered as their Christmas tree was put into place for decorating. This was a favorite family project. They always decorated the tree together on Thanksgiving evening. Everybody's favorite cookies and candies would be there along with plenty of hot chocolate and apple cider. It was so much fun to watch the children and grandchildren as they worked and laughed together. It was definatly the best time of the year for Rebecca and John Paul Cavender.

John and Rebecca always gave their children all expenses paid vacations for Christmas. It was a long standing and well known tradition, within their family. This year they had decided on a cruise to the Bahamas. It was scheduled for later in the New Year. Rebecca spent the next few days shopping for presents for her grandchildren. Their house would be filled with joy and love until the first of January, and then everyone would go back to their respective homes and jobs. Rebecca had promised herself that she wouldn't focus on John's situation until she had to. What in the world was happening to America, our great and wonderful country? Though she never voiced her concerns she secretly wished she and her husband could leave politics and be private citizens again. She knew this was wishful thinking on her part. John was a public servant. He loved politics, and she knew he was an honorable man. He was good for the country and would probably be president in a few years. The thought of being first lady did not appeal to her at all. She just wanted to be a wife, mother and grandmother. The lavish trips around the world she had enjoyed with John could not compare to the joy of their times at home with the family.

Rebecca was an only child. She was from one of the richest families in Texas. Her parents were very seldom at home so she was raised primarily by nannies and servants. Her childhood was so lonely, at times she wished they were poor so her mom and dad would stay home with her and they could be a family. That never happened as she was growing up so she was determined when she got married she would make her family a priority. She would focus on family and make hers the closest, and most loving, it could be. That was Rebecca's dream for as long as she could remember. The big house she had inherited from her parents was wonderfully filled with happiness when the family came together to celebrate the holidays. She had never had that as a child. Family was the most important thing in her life.

Rebecca met John in high school. It was love at first sight for both of them. When she met John's parents, she was instantly drawn to his mother Sara. She often said that Sara was the closest thing to a real mother she had ever had. She loved her very much. Sara was a sweet gentle woman, and filled such a void in Becky's life, that when Sara passed away Becky was devastated for months. Sara often spoke of Jesus. Becky, who had never been to church while she was growing up, learned a lot from Sara about faith.

John and Rebecca would soon be married thirty five years. She still loved him passionately. They had two children. John Paul the fourth and Sara Diane. They called John Paul J.P. And Sara Diane was called Diane. She was named for her grandmother and they were extremely close. Sara took Diane to church and Diane developed a deep faith in Jesus at an early age. She still held tight to her faith. She was a devout Christian, as was her husband Fredrick. J.P. married a lovely girl named Jillian, they have two children Alex and Adeline. John and Becky were extremely proud of their family.

CHAPTER FOUR

Grandmother's House

"Jillian are you and Alex about ready to go?" J.P. Cavender was in a hurry to get to the airport. He and his family were supposed to fly to Texas with his dad in Air Force Two. Their daughter Adeline was patiently waiting for the rest of the group. She was reading her favorite book of nursery rhymes, she would finish it on the plane. She couldn't wait to see her grandparents. Thanksgiving and Christmas were always great fun at their house. She and Alex would help Grandmother Becky with her shopping. She always bought them the neatest gifts. Adeline had a special gift for the two of them also. She had found a beautiful frame to put a copy of the constitution in. She had bought it in an antique shop where her mother loved to go. She had saved a long time for just the right gift for them. It would go great in their patriotic room. Grandmother was always decorating their home. Each room had a theme. The patriotic room was her latest creation. Grandfather loved this room. Of course, he loved everything about Grandmother Becky. They all did. She was a loving person and took wonderful care of her family. She was special that way.

Diane and Fredrick were also in route to the airport where they would join her father for the flight to Texas. Diane was humming one of her favorite Christmas songs. Mother will be in rare form this year she thought as the limousine rushed them to the airport. She was very proud of her father. Being the daughter of the vice president of the United States of America had its perks. They would be flying home on Air Force Two. Diane smiled as she thought about her mom. She knew she would be very busy; making sure everything was perfect for her children and grandchildren. Diane and Fredrick had a secret. They would tell the family over Thanksgiving dinner. Diane was pregnant again. They had wanted a child for so long. She had miscarried two babies. This time she was doing extremely well. She was well into her third month and so far no health problems. She and Fredrick had wanted to wait until the family was all together to tell them their good news.

John Paul knew he would have to talk to his wife and children soon about the seriousness of the vote he would soon have to cast. They had heard the rumors floating around Capitol Hill for some time. If the House passed their version of the bill, the Senate would certainly be divided across party lines. The Senate was equally divided, and of course as vice president he would cast the final vote. John had barely slept in weeks. He was torn over the decision he had to make. The Conservatives would fight to the last second to defeat this bill, but John knew the president was ready to sign the bill if it passed the Senate.

Rebecca could see the strain on Johns face. She knew he was concerned about the country. He could keep his feelings hid from the children, but not Becky. She went out of her way to show him how much she loved him. She had always made their homes a haven for him.

He could forget all his troubles when Becky was there. He decided he was going to enjoy his time with his family and worry about Washington when he had to.

CHAPTER FIVE

Thanksgiving

Thanksgiving Day was filled with the smell of food, and the bustling house was full of laughter, as the family sat down for their meal together. Diane was glowing and Fredrick stayed very close to her. Rebecca wondered if all was well with the kids. Diane seemed so happy that she decided of course all was well. Fredrick seemed unusually protective of his beautiful wife. Of course it was no secret that he loved her. He had since they met in law school. His law firm did a booming business. He was quite successful in his own right. Diane worked for a different but equally successful firm. They had a great life together. However Becky knew they both wanted a child very much. That would complete their joy.

The group sat down to a large feast. The cooks had outdone themselves this year. The turkey was golden brown and the fixings covered the whole table. Once they started passing the food the conversation started. They brought each other up to date on all that they were doing. The laughter was music to John and Rebecca's ears.

Suddenly, Alex spoke up. "Grandfather did you see the demolition of the big church on Fifth Avenue last week." A hush fell over the room. "It was so sad." Alex went on to say, remembering his mother's tears. "I have heard that many of our churches are being destroyed. Mom and I watched the whole thing. Grandfather, why are people angry with the church?"

John Paul knew he had to answer his young grandson. Obviously, this was upsetting him. He cleared his throat and started to speak. "I had hoped to wait until later to talk with you all about the changes that are coming if our government has their way."

"Many of the old churches are being condemned and torn down just like the one on Fifth Avenue. Others are being bought up by the government to be used for other purposes. There is a movement in this country right now to abolish the Christian Church. However the cry is getting louder, and the people with the money are crying loudest of all. As you well know it cost millions of dollars to run for office today and the lawmakers depend on these people to fund their elections. These same people are calling on the lawmakers to abolish the church. Our Constitution and especially The First Amendment has stood strong for over two hundred years and now there are those in Congress that say it is outdated."

When he was finished the room was silent for a long time. J.P put his hand on Jillian's as she started to cry. Rebecca felt as though the breath had been knocked out of her. Diane and Fredrick looked stunned and John Paul just bowed his head.

He continued, "I am so sorry to break this to you on Thanksgiving, but Alex had a right to have his questions answered honestly. The House and Senate are overrun with atheist. They are the enemy of Christianity. Also a great majority of the big contributors to the Liberal Party are unbelievers. They have been lobbying for years to overcome parts of the First Amendment to the Constitution that gives us our religious freedom. I'm afraid that we are approaching the establishment of a national religion. I'm not sure if they will call it atheism or political correctness or even secular humanism but more and more you are not allowed to disagree with these people. Our lawmakers are in the process of writing new legislation. They want to ban Christianity and anything that has to do with God in this country. They already made it illegal to display the cross outside of a church for fear of offending the Muslims. The churches of course are devastated. Some of the top ministers in our country are being threatened right now. The government has way too much power. We may soon all be enslaved by it."

Diane had been sobbing quietly, suddenly she began to cry out loud. Between her sobs she blurted out, "Fredrick and I are going to have a baby. Now I am afraid to bring a child into this world. We have always had our faith to help us when we were going through the pain of miscarriage. The church has been our strength. Daddy can't you do something?"

Rebecca was overjoyed and concerned for her daughter at the same time. She spoke up, choosing to focus on the joy. "Diane we are so happy for you and Fredrick. A new baby will be wonderful. We must not let politics ruin our day. We will deal with those after the holidays."

Then everyone started talking at once, they were all congratulating Diane and Fredrick on their baby news.

Once again, John realized why his wife was so special. He had never loved her more than now. She had a way of calming the fears of everyone around her, especially the children. He knew they would talk more about this later. He had big decisions to make. Somehow Becky's presence made him feel better. She was right he thought. There is nothing more important than the family. He felt better now that they knew what he was dealing with.

CHAPTER SIX

A Young Pastor Prays

L uke and Beverly Davis were kneeling at the altar of The First Baptist Church of Nashville. The young pastor and his wife were praying for God to guide them. Luke had received an anonymous letter that day. It was postmarked Washington DC. The sender informed the young pastor that a new federal law was being constructed to ban Christianity in America. Our lawmakers are busy at work right now. I thought someone ought to let the church know. Luke felt that God was sending a message directly to him. Luke had heard the rumors for a while. Their attendance was falling each week. People were afraid to come to church anymore. Some were even saying it was now against the law.

"Not yet," thought young pastor Davis. "The devil will never defeat our Lord. This is a battle that God will win. This is His church." The pastor suddenly remembered his father telling him that there was a time when they said the Lord's Prayer before school started each morning. He said no one believed that it would ever be any different. Today in America prayer can no longer be recited in our public schools. It is not legal to post the Ten Commandments in the court house anymore. The same commandments that our laws were based upon, can no longer be posted in public. Then he remembered how the atheist had wanted "In God we trust" removed from our currency. Always these groups were harping on "separation of church and state" as if it meant that nothing pertaining to God could be expressed in public and especially on public property. Somehow a statement from a letter that President Thomas Jefferson wrote to a group of Baptist who were concerned that the Congregationalist were becoming the state church. He assured them that the first amendment had erected a wall of separation between church and state. That letter which also stated that the government couldn't establish a national denomination also said that the amendment assured the free expression of religious beliefs. Now that phrase has been twisted to mean nothing religious can be done in public. Pastor Davis pleaded with God to do something to protect our Christian freedoms. He prayed for the people in his church. He asks God to give them courage and show them what to do.

Beverly had to leave to care for their children. As she left, Luke began to weep. His tears stained the alter. He stayed there on his knees all night. As the morning sun filtered through the stained glass windows, Luke Davis finally went home to get some rest. He was exhausted, but somehow he felt at peace.

Beverly knew her husband was very upset. She didn't know what they would do if their church had to close its doors. She knew Luke would fight to his last breath to make sure that never happened. The ministry was their life. Luke had been pastor of this church for ten years. Both of their sons had been born while they were here and each of them had been dedicated to God in this church. It was home to them. It was everything to the Davis family and now it was being threatened. Beverly knew that Luke hadn't slept all night. She had also spent the night praying. She was concerned for his health, but she knew that nothing would stop him from trying to protect the church.

By early afternoon Pastor Davis was up, refreshed, and looking for lunch. He felt as though he had slept eight or ten hours. He knew that God had a work for him to do, and praise the name of Jesus he was ready. After lunch Luke got on his computer and started e-mailing pastors all over the world. He asked them to pray without ceasing, and to start a letter writing campaign. He called every member of his congregation. He told them to be sure and come to morning worship on Sunday. He reminded them that their soul was in the hands of God and not the Government.

As he spoke to his members he could feel their courage coming back. He said, "We will not give up our right to serve our Lord. We must fight back this time. We have the power of the Almighty God on our side. Start praying," he told everyone, "And don't stop until the victory is ours. God will defeat our enemies. We will talk more about it Sunday morning." The next thing Luke did was to call his choir director with some special instructions. Then he called on all his deacons. He had a plan and it would take everyone to make it work.

CHAPTER SEVEN

Where are the Christians

Rebecca felt sad for the first time since Thanksgiving Day. January the First had come too soon for the whole Cavender family. As everyone said their good-byes at the airport and headed in different directions Rebecca headed to the house and John Paul headed to his office. The lawmakers would be back in town soon. When their new session started they would begin writing new law. John shivered at the thought.

"Where are the Christians?" he wondered. "Don't they care about this at all? Surely they're not going to take this lying down." He knew that his mother wouldn't. She would have taken a stand for Jesus. She would have opposed him if he voted against her religious beliefs. She would have died of a broken heart if this bill had become law while she was alive. One thing for certain it would never have stopped her from worshipping Jesus.

Suddenly his thoughts were interrupted by the intercom. "John can you come to my office? "It was the president.

"I'll be right there Sir," John replied.

The president looked a little worried. "John what do you hear about The Law?"

"Nothing yet" he told his boss. John had not always agreed with William, but he respected the office and was always polite. Well I expect it will be a battle over there. The Conservatives have let it be known they will not vote for any law that suppresses Christianity. Our contributors are applying pressure all over Capitol Hill. I get dozens of e-mails every day.

"I know, Sir, so do I. I hope they can thrash this one out without me."

William looked shocked. Why John, you wouldn't go against the party would you?

I never have, but this is something I've never had to be a part of. I'm not sure we need to stand against Christianity Sir. Why should we try to take away religious freedom? This country was built on the beliefs of the Bible and now we are saying to ban it. I find it very scary Sir.

"Well if I were in your position I would be concerned too. You are planning on running for president next term aren't you?"

"I was thinking about it, but this kind of makes it impossible.

William looked surprised. "Oh I don't know about that. John you would make a fine leader. Remember to promise the people whatever they want, and deliver as much as you can. They will vote for you every time…

"Thank you sir. I will consider all my options of course."

Both men had heavy schedules. Soon John excused himself and left for his office to go back to work.

CHAPTER EIGHT

Bad Times Coming

Luke Davis stood before a full congregation. "Thank you Jesus," he whispered. He prayed a prayer for guidance, and then spoke to the people in a soft voice. He said "I won't lie to you, there are bad times coming to the people of faith. The government is trying to take away our freedoms. They will get it done if we do nothing. I am here to tell you that I will fight to the death to keep that from happening. So now my question for you is this, who else is on the Lord's side today?"

"A wise man, Edmund Burke, once said, "All that is necessary for the triumph of evil is that good men do nothing." Christians have been guilty of doing nothing for a very long time. I need a few good people to pledge with me that they will do anything and everything that is legal, to take a stand for Jesus. We will have signup sheets after the service. We need your contact information so we can keep you informed. Also be sure to list any special skills that you would be willing to use to protect our Christian freedoms. Everyone here can at least tell their neighbors and friends that it is time to get serious about Jesus and His Church, before it is outlawed in this country."

Then he turned the service over to his choir director. The choir had selected praise songs for the service. They also planned a few old hymns. As they raised their voices in praise, the Holy Spirit came into their presence. The Church was alive and well. Pretty soon folks were crying and begging God to forgive them for running away. That morning they renewed their covenant with Him. Soon they were all making plans and signing up to take a stand for Jesus.

By the next Sunday the congregation had nearly doubled. The choir kept singing God's praises and the people kept working. The wonderful way they came together was an inspiration to Luke. He prayed for them daily and was blessed with many new members. The e-mails were flooding Luke's computer. Beverly was trying to keep track of all the correspondence. Her secretarial skills were certainly paying off now.

Many pastors were asking Luke to head up a seminar. One very inspired pastor wrote that it was important they all be on the same page. Luke decided to do just that. He would hold a seminar. He knew they needed to coordinate their efforts. He rented the largest building he could find. He sent out invitations to hundreds of pastors and announced it in every form of media they could think of. The next few weeks were the busiest the young pastor had ever seen. The ministry at the First Baptist Church was growing daily.

"Busy people are happy people," his choir director had told him. He was right. The donations had doubled at the church, and now funds were coming in from all over the country. Luke and his deacons carefully laid out a program for the seminar. He told them that this was an unplowed field. "We must never look back or waver in our convictions. Pray diligently for direction and listen carefully to the voice of God. I don't claim to have all the answers, but I trust that God will guide us as we trust him."

The announcement of the seminar was excitedly passed among the Christian community but largely ignored by the main stream media. They had a totally different agenda. On Monday, January the Fifteenth the New York papers printed the first article. They said that soon the Christian fanatics would have to shut up in this country. The Law, as they referred to it would put a stop to their openly preaching Jesus. The people in this country have spoken, they reported and the majority want to be free from Christianity. According to the article you can believe what you want to, but you can't try to lead others in that direction. You could go to jail for preaching openly. Churches will be banned from assembling folks together. The Bible will no longer be sold in this country. If you have a Bible you can only use it privately.

The House would vote on The Law next week and if it passes there, it will go to the Senate. President William Noble has already said he would sign it into law. From that day on the news was filled with, The Law as they had all come to call it. The Law was front page in every newspaper in the country. It was the lead story on every news channel. The people on the streets spoke of little else.

CHAPTER NINE

The Lord's Army

John Paul was a troubled soul. Even his family was divided on the subject. J.P. said he could care less if he ever heard another word about Christianity. Jillian was quiet on the subject, but lately she cried a lot. The Government was buying up the near empty buildings and tearing down the more conventional looking ones and remodeling the more contemporary looking ones into office spaces. Diane and Fredrick were devout believers. Rebecca never voiced an opinion, but he was sure she didn't like the idea of making any religion illegal. What she didn't say was that she was following closely a story that was coming out of Nashville. It seems a young pastor there was taking exception to the idea of "The Law." It appeared the Christian's were being quiet, but there was definitely something going on. She heard there was a huge seminar being planned and Fredrick and Diane were signing on as legal counsel for the group.

"Oh John," Rebecca thought "Please be careful." Right now everything was in the planning stages, but Diane had confided in her and asked her not to tell anyone just yet. They were being very quiet about who they were. They didn't want to do anything to bring reproach on John at such a critical time. Diane said her dad would always follow his heart. She had to follow hers also.

Luke sat down at his computer to answer his e-mail. It was overwhelmingly a positive response, though every now and then it was quite negative. As he read closer he realized there were some terribly violent threats being made against him. He had heard from some of the other pastors they were facing the same thing. He had said it weeks before and he meant it, nothing short of death would stop them this time. The Christian world had been passive long enough.

Over the next few days there were many threats. Bomb threats and a few actual bombings were carried out in some of the southern churches. The more they were threatened the stronger their resolve become. The church was rising up like a mighty army. They started planning a march to the Nation's Capital. They were writing and calling their Congressmen every day, all day long. Mostly it fell on deaf ears, but every now and then they received a response. They began to figure out who was for them and who was against them. They made lists and sent them to newspapers all over the country. Most didn't bother to publish them, but occasionally someone other than Christian outlets would publish them. The Christians started keeping track of who was refusing to publish their news releases and they started exposing them for their bias. No one was going to remain neutral on this and the Evangelicals were pledging to be at the poles in the next election and they would know who to vote for.

The word went throughout the nation that the Christians were going to march on Washington D.C. The news media descended on Pastor Luke and the First Baptist Church and soon they were on the nightly news. Luke had suggested that Beverly and the children go stay with her family, but she wouldn't hear of it.

She said bravely, "I am in the Lord's army, the same as you are, and so are our children. I trust God. He will take care of us or he will take us home. Anything would be better than living without the freedom to worship Him. This world is not our home, we are strangers here, but as long as we are here we must stand for Jesus."

After hearing his spunky little wife make that speech, Luke was more determined than ever to keep marching forward. The Lord was their strength and they would not turn back.

CHAPTER TEN

※

Luke's Seminar

The seminar was scheduled to start at seven o'clock. By five thirty the seats were filling up. Registration had filled up in just a few days. The crowd was primarily made up of religious leaders. Luke's planning group had anticipated the early arrivals and had a worship team leading the group in hymns to prepare their hearts for his message. Luke had expected to be nervous as he stood before this prestigious group. All that was quickly forgotten as he told them of the calling on his life. He had tears rolling down their faces as he told them that he believed there was a calling on their lives as well.

"God has spoken to me through prayer, through letters and through his word. He also gave me a little message through my wife."

He looked over at Beverly and smiled. She smiled back and he went on.

"We must stand together as one. Brothers and sisters alike. The time had come to be counted. We must overcome our denominational differences and stand as one for the Lord. Who is on the Lord's side tonight? Who will follow him, even to death if need be? As I read my Bible I am reminded that Daniel never swayed from God. He never gave in even when he was facing death. The same God that delivered Daniel will deliver us."

Luke told the pastors, "We all need to go to Washington D.C. and take as many with us as possible. We must let our voices be heard. We pay taxes. Many of these lawmakers were voted in by Christians and praise God Christians can certainly vote them out. They will not walk on the blood of Jesus and do it with my vote."

Like a heavenly chorus, "Amen, Amen," echoed loudly as it came from every corner of the large building. It was decided that first night that Pastor Davis would lead them to Washington and speak on their behalf. They didn't know exactly how to go about it, but they had a couple of young lawyers in the building that promised they would make all the necessary arrangements.

That night in Nashville, Tennessee revival broke out. As the speaking part of the night wrapped up, the Choir started singing songs of praise and worship. The Christians were on fire for God. That first night the pastors started talking about what was being planned. As they spread the word the excitement was contagious. People from all over the country started to show up to see for themselves what was going on. There was standing room only after that. Thousands came to Jesus. The "two day seminar" went on for a week.

"Washington D.C. here we come." was the message that reached John Paul's office that cold January morning. They want to be heard and they should be, he thought. He would do whatever he could to make that happen. He discretely called on his friends in the Conservative Party. He knew they would give the church a voice. The few close friends he called on would not reveal his involvement in this. They were glad that he was willing to help considering the position he was in. He gave them the letter he had received and they contacted Pastor Luke Davis. He was invited to speak before Congress the following week. The vote was being held up until a few more people could be heard on this new law. Congress always wanted to look good in the public eye, and the media was everywhere. The pressure was on each politician to commit one way or the other to The Law. Many who were against The Law were being threatened by The Law's supporters. John heard from thousands each day from both sides. This was one of the biggest political showdown this country had ever witnessed.

For the next few days the Christian communication team was busy day and night. Meet us in D.C. was the message heard around the country. Luke stayed at the alter every minute he could. He was praying for guidance.

"Sweet Jesus," he cried "I want to go where you send me and do your bidding. Please lead your humble servant to do your mighty will. What a privilege, to serve the true and living God and to do his will completely." He prayed for the message he was to deliver in the name of God. He pled the blood of Jesus to cover and protect him. To give him strength and courage to face the road ahead. That night even as Luke was praying, churches were being burned to the ground. Preachers were being killed and congregations were being forced into hiding. It was evident to the Christian world that Satan would do everything in his power to shut them down and he had lots of human help in doing so. To Luke's delight the church was showing no sign of giving in. This time they would stand. They knew they had failed many other times. This time they didn't believe that a country as blessed as America would turn her back on the one her blessings came from.

Oh the changes had come slowly. Eliminating prayer from school, legalizing the murder of helpless, precious little babies, refusing the Ten Commandments a place in public. The very things that had made our country great and strong were slowly being taken away. When it all began the Christian community didn't believe that one voice could take away their children's right to pray in school, or that one woman could legalize abortion. Today we have come of age. We are no longer so naïve that we believe that the bad influences in our country can't do anything they decide to, while we just sit back and do nothing. Well, no more. We want our constitution and our rights to be protected. Whatever it takes, Lord, we will do. Night after night the churches were filled with people praying and praising God. They were growing stronger and more courageous.

On January the twenty-third, the great halls of Congress were filled to capacity. Media cameras were everywhere. They had all come to hear the voice of one man, who until a few weeks ago no one had heard of. Pastor Luke Davis would speak today on behalf of the Christians who opposed the The Law. As he stood to speak you could hear a pin drop. He was not afraid and as he spoke with great authority given him by God the house was silent. He reminded the honorable Senators that no power was greater than that of the Almighty. He told them they should be ashamed of selling out for a few pieces of silver. Were they no better than Judas? He promised that anyone who voted for such an evil law would answer to God Himself. He reminded the Senators that Christians were good citizens, taxpayers and voters.

"You will not take away our freedoms anymore. Not without a fight anyway. Our Forefathers fought and many died for this right. This country was founded on Christian beliefs. God has blessed us and we are not giving up. We the people still make the decisions as to who will represent us, and rest assured we will bring out the vote. We serve a living God, and we will never deny Jesus, nor give up our rights to worship Him. The decision is up to you to make the law, but it's up to us to obey it. Rest assured we never will obey man's law when it goes against God's law; and if you were smart you wouldn't either."

The battle lines were drawn and everyone understood their positions. Some of the Senators were deeply offended. Who did he think he was to threaten them with a God they didn't believe in? At least they said that they didn't, but some of them were not so much convinced as they were bought and paid for. There were thousands of Christians in Washington that day. They promised they would be back for the vote.

CHAPTER ELEVEN

❋

Faith, Stronger than the U.S. Senate

John Paul sat in his office smiling, as he listened to C-Span to hear the young man speak. He wondered if the president had heard him. He also wondered how the young man knew his private address. The letter he received had come to his home. When his phone rang, he knew it would be The President.

Can you believe what went on today? The Christians showed up in full force. Thousands they estimated. One of them told the press they might not have a lot of money, but it didn't cost anything to vote. Man they are serious about this law. I'm not sure they should go on with this.

"Why William?" John asked a little amused; "You said you'd sign it. You've committed yourself."

"I know, and I think I'm starting to regret it now."

John just laughed and told the president he was late for a meeting. He'd discuss it more with him later.

The liberal machine went into full battle mode. They had to find out who this guy was, find some dirt on him and shut him up. He had a huge following. They could only hope he had a skeleton or two in

his closet. If they couldn't find something to use against him, they would have to make something up. The media loved this guy, but they knew how quickly the media could turn on you. They needed a story to turn momentum back in their favor. Any story good or bad. They were easy to manipulate. The way I see it, one Senator told the others, is he isn't well enough known to be too much trouble. The others weren't trusting that. They had all heard him speak. The truth was he was stronger and more courageous than all of them combined. They knew this was the time to play dirty if necessary and no one could do that better than they could. It didn't take much courage to sneak around, lie, and pay people off to spread lies. To attack from the background with the cover of "reliable sources." They could all do that quite well.

John Paul was actually laughing as he turned into his driveway. I've needed this for a while he said to Rebecca as he filled her in on the day's activities. This young preacher called the whole Senate a bunch of Judas's if they voted for such an evil law.

"Why, John Cavender, I do believe you are enjoying this" Rebecca teased.

"Well the young man has guts. I believe he meant every word he said. I know this is no laughing matter. It troubles me more each day. I believe the worst is yet to come. That young man embarrassed some Senators today. They won't take this without retaliation. I'm expecting an all-out attack. You know how dirty they can be. You wait and see."

"You are right I'm sure." Rebecca said.

The tone in John's voice had changed. She knew he was worried about the The Law and now she was too. She spent a sleepless night thinking about what John had said about retaliation. The sun had only just begun to lighten the sky when she picked up the phone and began to dial.

Luke had hardly opened his eyes when his phone started ringing. He didn't recognize the voice, but the person on the other end knew who he was.

"Pastor, please be careful. You have stepped on some toes in Washington. They will try to bring you down, so be on guard. I am a friend and I felt I should warn you. Bad times are ahead." Rebecca quietly placed the phone back on the hook. She had done all she could do. Even though she was in a very delicate position, she couldn't bear to think of that young man being harmed because he had the guts to stand for what he believed.

Luke was up and dressed in no time. He told Beverly he had to go to the church. He wanted to be alone and talk to God. As he prayed, he felt the Holy Spirit touch him ever so lightly on the shoulder. All fear left. He thanked God for hearing his prayer, said "Amen" and left the church.

The morning paper was full of the news about his trip to Washington. They said he made quite an impression on the Senate. The writer also said young Luke was a brave man to stand up to the Senators like he did.

Yes, Luke thought, and they will try to destroy me. I'm so glad my faith is in someone bigger and more powerful than the U.S. Senate.

CHAPTER TWELVE

It is a Set-Up

The Senators who supported The Law were very busy over the next few weeks. There were many closed-door meetings. All very hush, hush, rarely talking to each other publicly. When approached by the endlessly determined press they had no comment. The liberal machine was hard at work. They had spies everywhere trying to dig up dirt on the now very popular Pastor Luke Davis. When questioned by the media, they said only that he was wrong to try to mix religion with politics.

Luke was a busy man. He was constantly being called on by churches to explain The Law and what it would do to the church. He traveled all over the country. Usually Beverly traveled with him. Then, one frigid day in March, Beverly came down with a terrible cold. She begged Luke to go without her this time. She was feeling too ill to travel, but she knew the work must go on. He was scheduled to fly to Washington that weekend for a series of meetings. Reluctantly, Luke agreed to make the trip without her.

The phone call came almost immediately upon Luke's leaving his home. The spy who had been watching him let his boss know that Luke was traveling alone. This was the break that the liberal machine had been waiting for. They had searched in vain for something to use against him. Now was their chance to set him up.

Luke arrived in Washington early Thursday afternoon. As soon as he checked into his hotel, he showered and called Pastor Earl North. They already had a series of meetings scheduled with other pastors. They decided to meet for supper themselves and discuss the seriousness of this complicated situation they were all in. Pastor Earl had also arranged several speaking engagements for Pastor Luke. After supper they went to Pastor Earl's office. Luke went over everything with him one more time. The vote had been held up until May. They had a precious few months to strategize and get their people organized. The lawyers were working non-stop to defend the constitution and freedom. Thy settled on what seemed to be the best course of action to take. They prayed together as their meeting came to an end. Each man's faith in God helped to encourage and strengthen the other. They both were relying on God's promise that no weapon formed against them would prosper. Earl felt a slight uneasiness as he said goodnight to Luke. He told him to be careful as he left to return to his hotel.

As he drove all Luke could think about was The Law. He knew, of course, this would all end up in the Supreme Court eventually. Luke shuddered at the thought of that. The court was overwhelmingly liberal. He was beginning to say a silent prayer for the Supreme Court as he parked and headed for his room. He prayed continually as he walked across the lobby and rode the elevator to his floor. His mind was so preoccupied with all that was going on that he didn't even see the very young woman in the hallway until she bumped into him.

"I'm so sorry," she said.

"No harm done," Luke said and smiled at her. All of a sudden she threw her arms around his neck and kissed him full on the mouth. Luke was totally caught off guard. Before he could voice his objection, she turned and ran away.

"I wonder what that was all about" Luke said, out loud, with an amused look on his face. Later that night when he spoke to Beverly he told her all about his encounter with the pretty young stranger. They both laughed it off, not knowing what else they could do. Beverly knew her husband was faithful. He had never hidden anything from her.

The next morning as Luke left the hotel he was looking for the small cafeteria that Earl had recommended. Sure enough it was right next door. Suddenly the young lady appeared again. This time she fell into step with him as he crossed the parking lot. She was quick to apologize for her actions of the night before. He laughed and smiled at her as he told her how shocked he had been. She explained that she had mistaken him for someone else. He thought that was credible. It made more sense than anything he had imagined at the time. Something about running into her twice like this still seemed a little odd but Luke was a trusting man, so he asked,

"Are you hungry?"

"Starved" she replied with a charming smile.

"My friend recommended this diner. May I buy you breakfast?" He asked.

"That would be wonderful!" She exclaimed.

She's just a kid, he thought as he ushered her into a booth. She kept up a steady flow of conversation as she swallowed down a large order of pancakes. Luke asked her name. She told him it was Laura, then he told her his. He asked her if she were a Christian. She admitted that she had never been to church. For a fleeting moment the saddest look he had ever seen came over her face. She quickly regained her composure. After breakfast Luke excused himself and said he had a meeting to attend in about half an hour. He had to go so he bid her good-by paid the bill and left the cafeteria.

He never saw her again and forgot all about the incident, until a few days later when it came back to bite him hard. The media machine was in full force that morning, and the tabloid magazines were printing extra copies. It seems that young Pastor Luke Davis was something of a womanizer. Luke was on the phone with Beverly when the press started beating on his office door. They had some hard questions and when Luke asked what they were talking about they threw the pictures in his face. There he stood in front of his hotel room kissing an attractive young woman. Another pictured showed the two of them strolling down the street together, still another showed them eating breakfast together snuggled in a booth smiling and talking as though they were at the very least old friends.

Luke absolutely denied there was any wrong doing on either of their parts. He explained just what had happened.

"It was so innocent," He explained. "She was just a kid. I am a married man. I told my wife all about her. I would never be involved in something like you are insinuating. I bought her breakfast because she said she was hungry. You people can't seriously believe I would cheat on my wife and throw my life away for someone I've never seen before. I don't know this girl. I think I'm being set up by someone. I don't know who, but I promise you that God does, He knows the truth."

CHAPTER THIRTEEN

A Young Girl's Murder

Beverly was beside herself with worry. She had never seen Luke so discouraged. She knew he was innocent. Others, however, didn't know him like she did. Preachers started calling him to discuss the problem with him. Luke assured them that he had done nothing wrong. Most of them believed him. They knew it could happen to any of them at any time. So Luke's support didn't waver from his fellow Pastors. However even the Christian press that had treated him so well was now questioning his morals, and the secular press was in a feeding frenzy. They were printing every word they heard. They were quoting "reliable sources," and the stories were getting so wild that Luke didn't even recognize them. Luke knew God was with him, but he had never faced anything like this before. He knew that Satan was working against him and why. He knew he would have to keep on trusting God to deliver him from this situation. In the meantime his work was suffering under the influence of wicked people. Still Luke would not quit. He told the truth and then he refused to talk about it any longer.

Laura Johnson was getting ready to leave Washington. Her job was finished. Fifty thousand dollars had been sent to her hotel room by an anonymous donor. She had been featured in every supermarket tabloid there was. She was beginning to think she hadn't been paid enough for this job.

The Herald Newspaper was begging Dan Fontane for more stories on the shamed Reverend Davis. Dan hadn't been as hard on Luke as some of the others. He believed the guy was telling the truth. Why would someone in his position do something this stupid? Besides Dan really liked Luke. He kind of wondered if he were being framed by the liberals who hated Luke after he confronted them on The Law they were trying to get passed. Dan had been a newspaper reporter for a long time and he could usually smell a rat, and he thought something about this stunk to high heaven. He finally called Luke and asked if they could talk off the record. Luke agreed and invited him over for supper. Beverly was a good cook. She made a wonderful supper of fried chicken, mashed potatoes, green beans and rice pudding. For the extra touch she whipped up a batch of her buttermilk hot rolls. Dan arrived at six o'clock sharp. He had brought Beverly a beautiful bouquet of spring flowers.

"Thank you Mr. Fontane," Beverly said, as he handed her the flowers. She quickly put them in a vase and placed them in the center of the dining table. They added a cheerful atmosphere to the room. Beverly loved flowers.

Luke shook hands with Dan and invited him to sit down. Soon they were enjoying the food and having a deep conversation.

"I believe you Luke" Dan said. "I have been thinking about doing some investigating. "Would you be ok with that?"

"Absolutely" Luke said. "I have nothing to hide. I've done nothing wrong."

"I can't promise you anything, "Dan said,

"But I will do my best to get to the bottom of this and clear your name. Someone is out to hurt you and I intend to find out who, and why."

After Dan left, Luke and Beverly talked for a long time. That night Luke was able to sleep for the first time since all of this began. He knew that Dan was sent by God to help him. He was very thankful.

At the same time that Dan and Luke were talking, Laura Johnson was on a flight to New York. She wanted to see the sights of the big city and relax for a while. She didn't notice the tall blonde man sitting directly behind her. She had no idea that he had been hired by someone to take her out. She didn't know who had hired her so there wasn't any danger of her telling that, but if she even admitted that she was hired to do a job it would expose the lie. That made it too dangerous for her to remain alive. Two days later her body was found. She'd been shot in the back of the head. She probably never knew what hit her. Her purse was found next to her. It contained no money at all, just credit cards and her driver's license.

Dan walked into the Morning Times office uninvited. He smiled at the lead investigative reporter and asked if they could talk for a while.

"Well Dan, it's been a long time since you've been around. This must be important. Grab a seat and let's talk. It's really good to see you." Dan and Jeff Lewis went back a long way. They were good friends in college and still remained so twenty years later. Just as they were getting started Jeff's phone rang. He turned to Dan and said,

"Let's get out of here." They left the office and got into Jeff's car. He told Dan that there had been a homicide on the east side of the river. It looked like a contract job. Professional hits were usually very clean, no shell casings and little or no evidence left behind. They were usually hard to solve. This time the victim was so young it didn't make sense that someone would want her dead. She certainly wouldn't be a threat to anyone. As soon as Dan saw her he knew who she was.

"Jeff this is the girl who claimed to be a one night stand with Pastor Luke Davis. I know he didn't have anything to do with this. Someone is framing him and my guess is that she knew too much."

"Is that the young Pastor from Nashville who has taken on the government?"

"That's exactly who he is. I believe he is innocent, and that's one of the reasons I came to see you. With your connections we could quietly investigate this and break the real story. Our Government is corrupt. We both know that. It is the best government that money can buy"

"I would like to know why this beautiful young girl was shot down like an animal." Jeff replied. "We could work this one together my friend."

"Thanks Jeff I was hoping you would say that. I know I can count on you to be discrete. I'm afraid if we are not real careful, evidence will be destroyed. I have a feeling that is why this young girl died. I think we should go talk to the police and see what they know."

"Good Idea," the police captain and I have a good relationship. I think she will help us all she can as long as we work with her and not against her. She's a good detective herself."

"This smells of corruption and we can all benefit from finding out the truth. There could be a bombshell of a story in this. Who knows maybe we can be good Samaritans for once and help clear a good man's name?" The two friends parted company and promised they would start to work right away.

Luke got the news by phone." Poor kid," he said. "They used her, and then they killed her. She was so young I don't know how she could have known such unethical people." Luke prayed for her family and asked God to reveal her killer. He knew this was all out war. Satan was determined to destroy God's work and Luke knew for the first time in his life that he could be in real danger.

Beverly had awakened in the night. She felt such fear come over her that she actually got up out of her bed. As she sat in her darkened living room and prayed, she knew that God was speaking to her. Her home was not safe anymore. She knew she had to take the children to safety. The time had come to protect them. They were getting death threats every day now. Home was supposed to be a refuge but now it was just a very scary place. She feared it was only a matter of time until some crazy person would act on the threats. She had asked God to lead her and she believed the warning of trouble ahead was from God. Beverly started packing suitcases. She would leave at daylight.

It was a beautiful day when Beverly left with the children. The birds were singing and the earth seemed so serene. Her parents were thrilled to have the grandchildren for a visit and they begged her to stay also. She said she wouldn't leave Luke alone. She knew he needed her more than the children did right now.

"Oh God." she prayed, "Please keep us safe and Lord, keep us courageous." Beverly knew that cowards had no place in this battle. As she drove back home she kept remembering a little song that she had learned as a small child.

She started to sing, "I may never march in the infantry, ride in the Calvary, shoot the artillery, I may never fly o'er the enemy, but I'm in the Lord's army." She had a long drive ahead of her, but time passed quickly as she sang and talked to Jesus.

CHAPTER FOURTEEN

A Home and Church Destroyed

Beverly had indeed left at daybreak. Luke had taken the opportunity to go to his office to catch up on work that he had fallen behind on while he was traveling. He realized he wasn't hungry yet so he would work until he felt hungry. He was so engrossed in his work that it hadn't dawned on him that he was starving when he heard the blast. Luke bolted out the door. He knew the explosion sounded close and he ran around the corner of the church and turned toward his house. He suddenly stopped running. The total devastation before him was too much to comprehend. He said a prayer of thanks that Beverly had left so early to take the children to her parent's house. The parsonage that he shared with his family had been blown to bits. The street was filling with spectators. He could hear the sirens as the fire and police departments responded. People were trying to talk to Luke, but he was in a daze. He heard voices but he wasn't comprehending anything. He was totally overwhelmed as the seriousness of what was happening began to sink in. Soon the press was all over the place.

Dan Fontane was speaking with Luke when the next blast occurred. The shock wave actually knocked a few people off their feet, and the heat from the fireball was shocking. It was the church this time and in spite of the heat, Luke felt a chill come over him. Someone wanted him dead. If the church had detonated first he would have been killed. He had been totally engrossed in his work in the office at the time of the first explosion. He thanked God again that Beverly had taken the children to her family. At least they were safe for now. Luke wished Beverly would stay there too. He knew she wouldn't, she would stand by him no matter what he faced. Dan quickly took Luke aside and offered to help him in any way he could. Dan had a cottage in the mountains. He told his friend Luke he would be safe there.

Luke had tears in his eyes as he thanked the kind reporter.

He said, "I will have to wait here for Beverly, but I will consider your generous offer." Dan patted him on the shoulder.

"Luke you have a lot of friends and were not going anywhere."

"That means a lot to me Dan. I appreciate all you are trying to do to help us, but please you be careful too my friend."

Luke wanted to be alone so he could pray. He told Dan he would talk with him later. Luke was overcome with emotions. He felt thankful that his family was safe, but he also felt alone. He couldn't exactly explain it maybe it was that his home and church were both gone. As he started for his car a police officer grabbed him abruptly.

"Luke we need to check out your car before you drive it. The bomb squad will be here soon. You can sit in my car where you will be safe until they come."

Luke gratefully accepted his offer. As he sat there alone, he prayed earnestly for his Heavenly Father to guide him. He cried as he thanked him for keeping them safe. He knew it was Satan's intention that they were all supposed to die. The people responsible for this had carefully planned everything, but they weren't counting on God's protecting his family. Luke thought of young Laura Johnson. He knew now that they had used her to set him up. She was probably just a nice kid. He thought about how she must have been terrified if she knew she was going to die. He begged God to console her family, and to keep his protective hand on his family. Soon Luke felt better. He knew he should call Beverly but he would have to borrow a phone. He didn't have one any more. He returned to his church to see how much damage had been done.

The fire chief put his arm around Luke's shoulder in a fatherly way. "Son, I'm afraid it's gone. I hope you have good insurance. This is one of the worst fires I have ever seen. The whole church is burning to the ground. There really isn't any way we can save it. They must have planted a lot of explosives to make this big of an impact. Son if you need somewhere to stay for a while I have an extra room in my house. My wife would be glad to have you and your family stay with us until you can figure out what to do."

It was late afternoon when Beverly arrived. She was horrified at what she saw. Luke's warning had not prepared her for this. Her beautiful home and the church were both gone. She fell on her knees and cried out to God. She was so thankful that he had warned her to take her children to safety. Suddenly she heard Luke's voice calling her name. She quickly got to her feet and ran into his arms and they cried together.

As evening approached, more people showed up with offers of housing. There was enough donated food to feed an army. Almost every person that stopped by promised to keep them in their prayers. There were many donations of money to help them get back on their feet, and so many more personal donations that they knew they would never be able to thank everyone. The goodness of the people overwhelmed them.

The picture went viral and was reprinted in publications all over the country. Dan had captured the moment that Luke and Beverly had embraced against the backdrop of the burning church. It symbolized the turmoil the whole country was engulfed in, the battle between good and evil. The Christian community rallied quickly.

CHAPTER FIFTEEN

The Royal Suites Hotel

The news channels were fighting for the first interview with the Pastor. Dan had written a gripping story. He told the public about the death of a young woman, and how she had been used and then murdered. He told his readers that the Pastor was a victim of a "left wing conspiracy."

He said, "I have been a Liberal all my life, but I'm beginning to believe our country needs change. It's a shame when you can't disagree with the government without being murdered." He told his readers that he believed that Christianity was under attack and everyone needed to let their lawmakers know how they felt about it.

Jeff was busy in New York searching out evidence in Laura Johnson's homicide. The Police Captain had shared all the information she had with him. She was in the process of getting a court order so she could check out Laura's bank account. Dan sent Jeff his story and he printed it in The Times. The picture of the young pastor and his wife embracing and crying was heart wrenching. The pictures of their destroyed home and church were terribly sad. The readers responded. Letters filled the Capital Mail Room. Capitol Hill was on high alert. The people were angry. They blamed the liberal left for the despicable actions taken against this young pastor and his family. The White House Staff could not keep up with the calls, the e-mails, and the wires coming in. It seemed the whole country was outraged.

John Paul left his office to go home for the day. He wondered if the president was as shaken up as everyone else was. The country was demanding that he do something. John knew Rebecca would be upset. John had found out from Rebecca that Diane and Fredrick were helping the Pastor. As far as they knew, no one knew she was his daughter. John was proud of her. He knew she was doing what he had taught her.

"Always follow your heart," he whispered. He certainly would. John thought about his mother. She had taken Diane to church when she was small and after his mother passed away, Diane continued going to church. She reminded him so much of his mother. They both shared a deep commitment to Jesus. He really wished he had gone more and learned about Christianity. He knew Rebecca was a believer, but church had never been a part of their lives. Now it could be too late. He remembered his mother's Bible. It was worn with age and use. He decided it was time for him to take a closer look at the book that had been so precious to her.

Luke and Beverly were up early. The Royal Suits Hotel in town had given them a beautiful suite for as long as they had need of it. They checked in under aliases. The staff was informed that their whereabouts were to be kept secret. The media world was waiting for Luke to speak. They were all willing to cover it. Luke decided to call upon the other pastors and churches that had supported him. If the press wanted his story, they were going to do it on his terms. He wanted God to be praised in every circumstance.

CHAPTER SIXTEEN

Enemies of God

The big auditorium in town was donated this time and filled to capacity. The media from all over the world were clamoring to attend.

The group provided food for the tired press and then Pastor Luke spoke, "Ladies and gentlemen we are gathered here today to declare that Jesus Christ is still the Lord of Lords and the King of Kings. (Philippians 3:18-19 KJV... 18 For many walk, of whom I have told you often, and now tell you even weeping, that they are the enemies of the cross of Christ: 19 Whose end is destruction, Whose God is their belly, and whose glory is in their shame, who mind earthly things.) The enemies of God tried to destroy me and my family. They did manage to destroy our house and church building, but I'm here to tell you that both the church and my family are alive and well. We will rebuild the buildings and we will continue our efforts to protect the religious freedoms that this great country was founded on."

Then Luke did something on National television that surprised everyone. He asked that everyone who knew how to pray, to do so. He asked that they pray for their enemies.

He said, "Jesus died for them too. We don't hate you." He spoke softly to those who had tried to harm him, "We only wish you knew our Savior so you would never try to harm his word. He is greater than the whole world and no weapon formed against us will prosper. You will fail, for our God will not be denied. He created this world and it belongs to him. We are only visitors here and for the Christian we have Heaven to look forward to, (Philippian's 20 KJV- For our conversation is in heaven; from whence also we look for the Savior, The Lord Jesus Christ: but you, who are against God, will spend eternity in Hell. You will believe in him then, but it will be too late.")

The press hung on to every word, and the television cameras were focused on his face.

"In trying to defeat us" Luke spoke with great conviction. "God has opened up bigger doors and we are not afraid to walk through them." The next few weeks that message would be played over and over again on national television.

"What an awesome God we serve." The choir started singing as Luke finished his message. The world stood amazed. The church was getting stronger instead of weaker and people who never knew God were pulling out the old Family Bibles and taking another look. Interest in Christianity was booming. Before the week was out construction workers were clearing out the demolished church site to start rebuilding. Not only had the insurance paid off quickly, the people were sending generous donations of money from all over the world. They would be able to build a much bigger church now. Luke was never going to believe that God would allow these Senators to take away his freedom to worship.

The president had called a meeting with all the Liberal Leaders. The House and Senate Leaders were there along with the vice president, secretary of state, and many other members of his cabinet.

"What is going on with The Law? President Noble asked the leaders of the House and Senate.

Representative David Forman, one of the biggest supporters of the bill was first to speak. "We are planning to call the vote in May.

We are trying to wait until the country calms down some. We must try to get this passed this session or we may never be in power again."

"The Christian right is all riled up." The president reiterated. "They have a lot of voting clout. They will never vote for any of us again."

"That may not matter soon. You know how quickly they forget. They are not fighters. They will pray and move on as usual and we will have our law. Just as we planned." David said.

"I'm not so sure this will go away." John Paul spoke up. "This is leaving me in an awkward position. I might have run for president next term, since William's term will be up. The way I see it this is a recipe for failure. Why does this have to be done now? I receive hundreds of letters a week, not counting e-mails and wires. People on both sides of the aisle are offended by our actions."

"Maybe they are, but in time they will get over it. The Christians have run this country long enough. They fight everything we try to do for the good of the country. For example they are still trying to overturn Roe versus Wade. They disagree with a woman's right to choose abortion. They call it murder and we all know that it is not a baby yet. Their freedom to pray in school is still a sore topic amongst them, even though Madelyn Murray O'Hare is long dead and gone. They are still screaming about our stand on separation of Church and State. I have heard there is a movement to get the Ten Commandments back on federal property. What gives them the right to undo everything we have accomplished?" David felt very angry and he was going to oppose these fanatics every way he could as long as their party was in power.

"Furthermore, Mr. Vice President you may have to cast the final vote. Are you with us or against us?"

"I have never voted against my party, but I don't need this just as I'm ready to run for the office of president. This is not a good thing for me, and frankly, I do not see why we have to mess with this law at all. Many people are against it. What good can possibly come out of this? My friends I am very confused on the whole notion that our country is turning against God.

"John you are not one of them Bible toting fanatics are you?"

"No, but my mother was and she was the best person I have ever known.

"Well, you will have to decide where you stand, because I can assure you that the vote is coming down."

The president interrupted. "What is the hurry? "He addressed David.

"The people who support us are screaming for change. A large portion of our party is atheist. They say that God is a myth. That these fanatics are living in la-la land. We are in a position to actually do something about this. We may never have this chance again. Our party is in power, for the first time in years. You know it is now or never for us, and frankly we need the support of the people who are demanding change. I have never believed in this Christ stuff, and it's time to stop lying to the people."

"Do you really believe what you are saying, or is money influencing you?" John sounded angry as he asked."

"I have told you what I believe. We are ready to submit our bill. We expect the whole party will be in favor. Your office will be getting a copy in a few days. Of course the senate is split 50–50. Unless by some miracle one of the Conservatives vote with us, John, your vote will be the tiebreaker. We must have you on board to win this.

Abruptly, this time the president said the debate was over." You boy's know where I stand. We might as well get the job done." John left his office right after the meeting. He was tired. He could not remember ever being more tired than he was now.

CHAPTER SEVENTEEN

A Threatening Call

Rebecca could tell he was upset. Her heart went out to him. He really was a good man. She knew he was so confused that he didn't know what to do. She decided to plan a short vacation for the two of them. John loved the outdoors, and they owned a cabin in the Blue Ridge Mountains. She could send their maid and butler on ahead to get everything ready. She decided to go right after the first of the month. May was the month of wildflowers, her favorite time of the year for outings. John could fish and relax. There were beautiful mountain streams right near the cabin. She would ask John later, if he could get away. The phone rang and as Rebecca went to answer it, John came into the room. It was Alex.

"Grandmother Rebecca I would like to come visit you for a few days. Would it be alright?" She could tell by the tremor in his voice that something was worrying him.

"Of course Alex." How about the weekend?"

"That would be great. Could you pick me up or do I need to have mother and dad bring me over?

"Let me speak with your mother and she and I will arrange something."

"Great, thanks Grandmother."

"You're welcome dear." Soon it was all arranged. J.P. and Jillian would bring him by at six o'clock and they would eat dinner together. As she hung up the phone she turned to John and filled him in. Then she asked if they could take a short vacation.

"A few days away from here might do us both some good," she suggested. John quickly agreed.

The next morning, as soon as he walked into his office, the phone rang.

"Good morning" John said in a pleasant voice. He was sure it would be the president. He usually called very early in the morning.

The voice on the other end told him that they were watching him and his family and he'd better know how to vote. "We can always get to your grandchildren and your pretty wife."

"What do you want from me?" John asked as he flipped on his tape recorder.

"I want you to vote with your party. I will not be happy if you don't. I know your daughter is pregnant. You wouldn't want anything to happen to her and the baby, now would you?"

"Of course not," John spoke very clearly. "I always vote with my party,"

"That's a good thing especially this time. Oh and by the way keep this call between the two of us, or else."

John knew that he and his family were being threatened. Someone knew that he wasn't completely in agreement with his party. That didn't mean he wouldn't vote with them. After all he was a true Liberal. That afternoon he met with the president and told him he would be out of town for the next week or so. "Rebecca want's a little of my time." John said nonchalantly. For some reason he didn't want the president to know what was going on. After all he had the Secret Service detail who accompanied him wherever he went.

"Alright John, I'll see you when you get back. Stay in touch."

With that taken care of, John headed home. He wanted to see his family right away. He called Diane and Jillian and asked to see them that evening. He told them he was making reservations for dinner at the little restaurant near his office. He told Jillian to get a baby sitter for Alex and Adeline. "They don't need to hear what I have to say tonight."

Rebecca's face went white with fear as John told her of the threats against them. "John I'm scared," she whispered. "Not for myself, but for the children and grandchildren. Shouldn't we call the F.B.I.?"

"I will as soon as I speak with the children. They were threatened too."

"Was William threatened?

"He didn't say. Of course I didn't confide in him either. Let's go Becky, I don't want to keep the children waiting."

"The Blue Moon restaurant was filled with hungry customers. John loved the atmosphere. The blue lights that hung like big round moons gave it a warm touch. John and Becky arrived just as J.P. and Jillian were getting out of their car. It wasn't long until Diane and Fredrick joined them.

"What is going on Dad?" Diane asked as soon as they were seated. Just then the waiter approached their table and they all gave him their orders. As soon as he left John told them about the phone call he had received that morning. Diane the threat was on the entire family, but he singled out you and your baby.

"Dad why are we being threatened?" J.P. asked.

"Son, do you remember the talk we had at Thanksgiving about The Law they would be trying to pass in Congress this term?"

"Yes, something about banning Christian freedoms in this country. Like not allowing them to speak about it in public. Why is the AFA so determined to do this? What are they afraid of?"

"The extreme left wingers of the party are determined to pass this bill. The president says he will sign it into law. Although they know it will ruin my chance at running for president this next term they are determined to go ahead. In our last meeting with the leaders, I questioned the necessity of doing this right now. Someone got the idea that I might vote against the party, although I never have. This is dividing the country. Churches and their Pastors are under attack every day. These people are very upset at what our government is trying to do. Now the enemies of the church are threatening my family, and I believe they mean business.

"Dad you are afraid for us aren't you?"

"Yes, son that's why I wanted to see you all tonight. I told the president today that Rebecca and I would be busy for the next few weeks and I wouldn't be in the office. I have lots of time coming to me, so that's not a problem. We're going to the mountains for a while. I think maybe you should all come along until the F.B.I. can get to the bottom of this. Rebecca and I were planning to go anyway. So I decided after the call that maybe we all need to get away for a while."

"My schedule is flexible." J.P. said.

"So are mine and Fredrick's, Diane chimed in. When do we leave?"

"I thought we could leave Friday afternoon. Could all of you be ready by then?

"We'll be ready," they all spoke together.

"But mom," Alex whined, "Why can't we go to school today?"

"Your grandparents want us all to go on a little vacation with them for a few weeks. I have cleared it with your school. You and Adeline will be given plenty of time to make up any class work that you miss."

"That sounds like great fun" Adeline said. "I love to go on vacation with the family.

"Me too," Alex said, a big smile on his face now. His grandparents were the best, and Aunt Diane was always ready to play with them, or go shopping or do something fun. Adeline didn't mind taking a break from school. The private school where they both attended knew who their grandfather was and that there would be times when the children would have to be away for a while.

CHAPTER EIGHTEEN

Visiting the Children

Pastor Luke Davis was quietly at work. He would lead a group to Washington D.C. in a few weeks. They already had their supporters lined up, but each day the numbers were growing as more and more churches signed up to go. They would arrive the morning of the vote, and leave as soon as it was over. Each group would provide their own food and they would stay together. Luke would be speaking to the people from a podium arranged by their friends in Washington. They would call on all members of Congress to rethink The Law. Luke didn't know if it would do any good or not, but God was leading him and he knew God's word would never come back void.

Beverly was going to visit the children for a few days. The construction workers were busy rebuilding their home and the church. They would be back in their home by the first of July. Luke had heard from his lawyers that morning. They would not be available for a few weeks. They said they were being threatened and so would have to lie low for a while. They also said that they would keep in contact and do whatever they could undercover.

"Our parents and sibling are also under this threat. We know how important this work is and we will be there at the necessary time. We are also preparing a lawsuit against the government. The constitution protects against what they are doing. We will be ready to file it immediately after the vote in Washington if they vote to take our rights away.

Dan and Jeff were busy helping the New York Police Captain search out leads in the murder of young Laura Johnson. It was Jeff's idea to look at the security tapes at the airport and on the airplane that took her from Washington to New York. The tapes revealed the young woman was being watched by a man with blonde hair and piercing blue eyes. The man's picture was already on the F.B.I. most wanted list as a John Doe. He was identified as a person of interest in several murders. After much investigating they had put a name to their person of interest. Their John Doe turned out to be James Carson. He had a lengthy criminal record. He had never been convicted of murder, but had been questioned in several. There had never been enough evidence to bring him to trial. The police in three states suspected that he was a gun for hire. Still no one had been able to prove it.

CHAPTER NINETEEN

In the Mountains

John and Rebecca were getting into their SUV when a car approached them. It was long and black. A tall young man exited the car. He was blonde and there was something strange about his eyes. He asked for directions to the White House. After John told him how to get there the young man said, "Thank you Mr. Vice President." With that he turned and got back into the car and left.

Rebecca was troubled by the whole exchange. "John did you know him?" she asked.

"Of course not, why?"

"It seemed to me he deliberately sought you out, and made a point of letting you know that he knew who you were.

"He didn't seem threatening," John observed.

"No I guess not, but after everything else I seem to suspect everyone that I don't know. John I know we are in danger so every stranger seems like a possible threat to me."

"I know sweetheart, and I'll feel better when we get some miles between us and D.C.

"We will be leaving in a few hours," Rebecca assured him.

The children would meet them at the airport at four o'clock. They would fly to within a few miles of their cabin and a car was arranged for them there. Everything was ready for their arrival the maid had put fresh linens on their beds and the kitchen was well stocked with food. The cabin sat high in the Blue Ridge Mountains. The views were breathtaking. Staying there always had a wonderful effect on John. He seemed more relaxed there in the mountains than anywhere else. That's why Rebecca had suggested they go there for vacation.

The next day John sat by his favorite trout stream. He was beginning to unwind for the first time in months. Rebecca had made him a sandwich and a thermos of coffee for lunch and packed them in a small cooler. John reached into his tackle box lifted out the upper tray and pulled out something that he had packed. It was his mother's Bible. Nobody knew he had brought it with him. As he carefully smoothed the pages he felt very close to his mom. As he read little notes she had made and scriptures that she had marked, he was amazing at the peace that come over him.

"My mom loved Jesus," He thought, "So he must be real. I don't understand why the country is so afraid of him. There is no other reason for the government to try to get rid of him." John felt a tear run down his face.

"Mom please help me," he thought. He continued to read for hours. Finally as the sun begins to set he carefully placed the Bible back in his tackle box and put his fishing gear away. He decided he would read as much of the Bible as he could before he voted.

That night John called the president. He had decided to confide in him since the Feds were involved now.

William told him how sorry he was. "John do you have adequate security where you are now?"

"Yes, we are fine. The family is enjoying a little vacation. I am most worried about Diane. She is expecting her first child and they were directly threatened. She's really vulnerable right now."

"I can imagine. John don't hurry back. I will call you on our protected line and keep you informed. By the way there was a strange fellow hanging around the White House. The Secret Service picked him up for questioning. He asked them about you. Of course he wasn't told anything, but I still thought you should know."

"What did he look like William?"

"We took a picture, he's kind of tall, with blonde hair and strange blue eyes. The video cameras picked him up all over the Capital Grounds. He may be a threat, we just don't know yet, but he will be in custody until we know for sure."

John told William that it sounded like the same guy who had confronted him the day he left for vacation. Rebecca didn't like the way he acted, but I just shrugged it off. He knew who I was and it seemed like he wanted me to know that he knew. Rebecca instantly reacted, I guess I need to be more observant."

As soon as they signed off John told Rebecca what happened.

"I knew he was up to no good," she said.

President Noble sat down to an early breakfast with the Speaker of the House, Charles Burns. He wanted to know if the House was about ready to act on The Law.

He said, "Charles this is becoming a dangerous situation." He went on to tell him of the threats made against the vice president and his family.

"Do you really believe you will be able to abolish religious freedom in this country?"

"We are going to try. We have the support we need in the House. The Senate might be a little tighter since it is split fifty-fifty. However our deciding vote will come from John and he will vote with the party. To answer your question I think it's now or never."

John sat down in the den and opened his mother's Bible. He was so interested in what he was reading that he couldn't wait until he was sure he was alone any more. He felt sure that Rebecca had noticed what he was reading but she hadn't let on. Today he started reading in the book of John. He didn't stop until he read the whole book. He was beginning to understand why his mom loved this book so much. He was sleeping much better now that he was away from Washington.

That night as they all sat down for dinner he made a startling announcement. "I am seriously thinking about walking away from politics after this term is over."

"What will you do Dad?" J.P. asked.

"I haven't decided that yet. I just don't care for this anymore. I want to do something where I can make a difference. I may start a foundation of some sort. I have a few ideas and I know my Becky would like nothing better than to go home to Texas and live the family life she loves so much."

Rebecca loved her husband so much, and he was right, but she knew his country needed him more right now. She would wait, her time would come. John would be a great president and she could not deprive her country of his leadership.

As they lay side by side later that night she asked John if he were really considering leaving politics. He assured her he might have to.

"What do you mean john?" she asked.

"Well you know how bad, things are in Washington right now. As a rule I don't let it get to me but when my family is threatened by people who support my own party, I can't tolerate that. I've been a Liberal all my life, but I'm more of a moderate. The party has swung so far to the left I don't know if I am a Liberal anymore or not."

"John you can run as an Independent or you can change to the Conservative party if that's what you need to do. I will always support you. However you must follow your heart on this vote. I will never tell you how to do your job, but never go against what you believe, party or no party. We still have the freedom to choose."

"If we start taking away the freedoms of others. No one will be free anymore," John mused.

"You are right John so think carefully before you commit yourself. We love you, and we believe in you. No matter what happens we will stand by you."

He held her tight as they fell asleep. She had always been his best friend and number one supporter, and he loved her more than anything else in the world.

CHAPTER TWENTY

A Baby is Born

"**M**other, wake up," It was Diane.

"What's wrong dear?" Rebecca was still half asleep.

"Mother I'm starting labor" she cried. "And I'm only eights and a half months."

"John, wake up, we have got to get Diane to the hospital."

Fredrick appeared in the doorway with Diane. He was grinning from ear to ear. He held Diane's suitcase in one hand and the baby's bag in the other. "Come on people, I'm going to be a daddy today." He smiled at his pretty wife and whispered, "And you are going to be a mommy."

All of a sudden everyone was getting ready in a hurry. John called the hospital to let them know that they were on their way. They had made arrangements just in case her labor started while they were here in the mountains

J.P. told them to go on and he and Jillian would bring the children a little later.

Adeline was yelling, "I want to go now auntie Diane. I'm going to be a cousin."

"What a wonderful family we are," laughed Rebecca.

Diane was scared. This would be her first delivery and the baby seemed to be coming a few weeks early. The ride to the hospital was a lot longer, and Diane thought a little bumpier, than it would have been from home. As soon as they arrived the doctors assured her that the baby should be fine. Still with her past history she was a little uneasy. Rebecca was right by her side encouraging her as only a mother can. John was taken to a private waiting room where the family could stay while they waited on the arrival of the baby. Fredrick was inseparable from Diane. He was beside himself with fear and anticipation and trying his best to keep his fear from showing.

J.P. and the rest of the family soon arrived. The children totally excited, especially Adeline who was rooting for a girl cousin. Diane knew she wouldn't be disappointed. They had known the sex of the baby for a while. They had kept it a secret. It was something they could privately enjoy for a while. She and Fredrick had relished every moment of this pregnancy. The only dark cloud was the threat of The Law. They were determined to do whatever it took to stop this insanity.

At five thirty pm on May the first, baby Rebecca was born. She what a beautiful sight. Her grandmother was in a state of shock when she found out that the baby would have her name.

"It's a bible name," Diane whispered to her mother. Rebecca never knew that. John was so happy for his family. A new edition to an already wonderful loving family. He had never seen Rebecca happier. She was bubbling over with pride. Her namesake was as beautiful as the one whose name she carried. John hoped she would always be as beautiful on the inside as her precious grandmother was.

Adeline was waiting patiently, or at least as patiently as possible for a girl her age, to hold her little cousin. She was as proud of this baby as if it were hers. Adeline had decided she would give the baby her favorite book, "Winnie the Pooh." She knew that baby Rebecca would love that book as much as she did. Nothing could take away the joy this family felt right now. They would face the rest of the world later, but this was their family time and they all embraced it.

CHAPTER TWENTY ONE

A Sudden Death

Luke and Beverly were running a little late that morning. Church was being held in a rented building. The new sanctuary would be ready by the end of summer. Luke was so proud of his congregation. They had risen to the challenge and soon they would be in their new church.

Dan had called Luke with some news. The Feds had found the guy who had followed Laura Johnson to New York. They were sure he had murdered her. They thought he had threatened the vice president and his family as well. They weren't giving out a lot of information, but Jeff and Dan felt sure he was a hired gun and they intended to find out who hired him. He wasn't talking to anyone except his lawyer.

Luke was glad he had been apprehended. He wondered if the same people were behind the bombing of his church and home. They were trying to kill him and his family. He wondered why they would go after the vice president. He would request the congregation to pray for the leaders of this country. He knew they really needed prayer. Luke had several scheduled meetings in Washington next week. Maybe he could get some answers there. The Christian groups were keeping their ears to the ground. They had friends as well as enemies in the senate. It seemed this was a test of the powers of good and evil. Luke prayed for his enemies as well as his friends that morning. He knew the vice president was in turmoil over The Law. His lawyers had told him so. They knew a lot about the politics in Washington. He thanked God that they were on his team.

Alex was unusually quiet. He had hoped for a boy cousin. He did think the baby was kind of cute. He guessed he'd get used to her in time. Maybe his mother could have another baby and get him a brother. Oh well, he decided to just enjoy the moment with the rest of the family.

Beverly was going to visit the children while Luke was in Washington. She had wanted to go with him, but he insisted on going alone. He feared for her safety. He knew Beverly would follow him anywhere, but she was needed by their children.

"Have a good trip," she told Luke as she left to go to her parent's home. Luke remembered her smile all the way to Washington. She was a beautiful woman. He said a prayer for her as she traveled. He didn't know the trouble she was headed for.

Beverly liked to take side roads when she could and the trip to her childhood home was filled with them. The air smelled of honeysuckle as she drove along. She turned on her CD player and sang along with her favorite gospel groups. Beverly loved to sing. She never did it in front of anyone, but she always sang in the car. Her favorite song was "Oh How I Love Jesus." She smiled as she thought of Luke and his mission. Beverly noticed a car following closely behind her, but she didn't think anything about it. She was still singing her heart out when the car suddenly sped up and sideswiped her car as it passed. Beverly lost control and her car went over a fifty foot embankment. The driver of the other car never slowed down. It was several hours before her car was discovered. Beverly Davis was dead.

Luke answered the phone in his hotel room. It was his Head Deacon Robert Clark. "Pastor come home, Beverly has had a very bad car accident."

"Is she alright," Luke wanted to know.

"I'm afraid not. She was killed. I'm so sorry." The deacon was crying.

Luke assured him he would return on the next flight available. He was so numb he could barely function. He somehow managed to call his host to let him know he would be leaving. One of the pastors who had invited him was soon at his side.

"Luke, I have called the airport and booked your flight. You can be home in about three hours. I will fly with you. You shouldn't be alone now." It was Pastor Bill Nelson. He secretly wondered if Beverly had been murdered. So many Christians were being killed. Some people said the country was on the verge of a civil war. The Christians were being attacked on every hand. This was a war he suddenly realized. Whether the Christians acknowledged it or not the other side was at war with them. Then he looked at the young pastor. In only a few months he had lost everything he owned and now even his wife was taken from him. Pastor Bill started to pray, "Oh dear God, Please help this young man who serves you every day. Please help him in his hour of need."

Luke's mind was in a fog for the next few days. "Oh God," he prayed. "Help me to understand this. My beautiful Beverly. She never hurt anyone in her life and now it looks like someone deliberately ran her off the road and killed her. Why? Why? Why?" he sobbed into his pillow that night. The funeral service was scheduled for the next day. There were so many people offering their services that Luke finally turned it over to his deacons. The only request he made was for the choir to sing her favorite song. The flowers and cards flowed in from all over the country. The media was everywhere. Dan was speaking on behalf of the family. He had volunteered and Luke gratefully accepted.

"Lord, I am so weak," he cried. "I love her so much and I can't imagine life without her. Father please help my babies. It will be so hard for them without their mother. She was so special. Why would anyone want to harm her?" Luke struggled with these questions day and night.

A few weeks after the funeral Luke heard from his lawyers in Washington. They had sent him a letter of condolence. They offered to help him in any way they could. Fredrick and Luke had gone to college together. They had gone in different directions after school, but they remained friends. Luke had decided on the ministry and Fredrick headed for law school. When Fredrick first contacted Luke he had confided Diane's relationship to the vice president to him and asked that he keep her identity secret. He told Luke that they wanted very much to help him as they were both devout Christians. Luke had kept their secret. He knew the position they were in and he loved them very much for their willingness to give him legal counsel in spite of their circumstances. They were brave and now Luke knew that he must be brave too. The vote would be in two weeks. "God don't let my Beverly's death be in vain." Luke was praying for victory, and knew it would only come through Jesus.

The Senate was struggling with the language of the bill, "They had to make sure there were no loop holes for the fanatics to wiggle through. They were an intelligent bunch even though they believed in myths and fairytales."

Soon the bill was ready for the vote. Copies were sent to the president and vice president. John felt sick as he read over the bill. It could be law very soon if something wasn't done. He called Diane and asked if she could come to his office.

"Sure Daddy, I'll come by for lunch."

As he hung up the phone, John had to smile. He knew she would come through the door with burgers and fries for them to share as they talked. Sure enough Diane showed up loaded down with food from his favorite little restaurant. All the things she knew her father liked. They chatted as they ate. John asked her about Nashville and her connections there. She filled him in on all they were doing.

She said "Daddy you know I respect your feelings and I hope you can respect mine. We are prepared to fight the government over our religious freedoms. I hope my position won't hurt you in any way. I just know I have to take a stand on this issue."

John assured her he understood, but once again he cautioned her to be careful. She promised she would.

The next day Diane sent a fax to Luke. She had invited him to come visit her and Fredrick for the weekend.

He faxed her right back and accepted her offer. Luke made a mental note to pick up a gift for the new baby. He had visited with Beverly's mom and dad the day before and they had asked if the children could stay on with them for now. Luke was thankful for their help. He knew they were as heartbroken as he was. The children were very happy where they were, and he got the sense that their presence was a comfort to Diane's parents. His schedule would be terribly hectic for the next month or so. He missed the children but he knew this was the best arrangement for now.

CHAPTER TWENTY TWO

Founder of the AFA

The main supporter of The Law was a man named Milton Borsch. He was the founder of the AFA (The American Freedom Association) He was a devout atheist and filthy rich. Half of the Senators in office today owed their jobs to him. He had financed every one of their campaigns to the tune of millions. Today he had The President on the phone. "Listen William I am not happy with the way John is handling things. He is closer to the other side than you may think. I hear his Son-in-law is good friends with that Preacher over in Nashville. We are about ready to take him out."

"Milton I don't want to hear this from you. I think there has been enough bloodshed courtesy of your group."

"Look William I put most of you in office and I'll take you out too if I have too. You know the people who work for me are ruthless, but they do follow my orders. That is something I need to see more of in you politicians. I won't be made a fool. I have many others to answer to, so don't let me down now. The results could be deadly if you catch my drift.

William's reaction to Milton was physical, it was a mixture of anger and fear. He was feeling hot and clammy at the same time. "Milton I could end up in prison for even associating with you. I think this has gone way too far. By the way did you have anything to do with the death of that young preacher's wife over in Nashville?"

"I'll never tell, besides you don't want to know."

"I want the killing stopped right now and I mean it."

"William I don't take orders from you or anyone else."

That night Milton told his henchmen that he wanted young Fredrick taken out.

"I would take them both out but it may be too dangerous to touch the daughter of the vice president. She won't participate without Fredrick." Milton would never admit having anything to do with this one either. To Milton, Fredrick was just one more Christian he wouldn't have to deal with. Milton was a devil. He had no heart at all for anyone except himself.

William was sitting alone in the Oval office when his secretary came in to ask him to sign some papers.

"Excuse me for asking sir, but are you alright? You look very pale."

"I guess I'm just tired," he responded, "And this heartburn just won't go away. Would you ask Steve to come in here please?" Steve was the head of his Secret Service Team. He was both an employee and a loyal friend.

"What can I do for you Sir?" Steve didn't waste any time at all getting there.

"Steve, what I have to say must be kept top secret."

"You know you can trust me sir."

"You know who Milton Borsch is don't you?"

"Yes sir. Why?"

"He is a dangerous man. I believe he is having people murdered. I want you to keep an eye on him. If we can prove he is a killer we can discreetly turn him over to the F.B.I."

"Oh he is a murderer Sir. He was behind at least two deaths that I know of, and The Agency is trying to flush him out right now. He has made some enemies and a lot of mistakes. He is like a time bomb ready to explode. He thinks his money gives him the right to do as he pleases and for most of his life it has."

"Steve how do you get your information?"

"Sir, it's my job to know the people that come in contact with you. How else could I protect you?"

"Steve keep him under tight surveillance, and when you have anything, make sure the FBI is informed."

"Consider it done sir." Steve replied as he hurried off to implement his orders.

William made a mental note to give Steve a bonus. He was the best. William was still feeling clammy and suddenly he couldn't breathe. He clutched his chest and fell to the floor. His secretary heard him fall and came running.

John's phone rang about midnight. It was the White House.

"You must hurry John." It was the President's Secretary, "The President has been taken to the hospital and it doesn't look good." John quickly awoke Rebecca and filled her in. "I will call later and let you know what is going on." The Secret Service ushered him into his limo and two escort vehicles accompanied them to the hospital where they were met by others. Everyone was on high alert. He was totally surrounded by agents as he was escorted to The President's room.

When John left the hospital William was asleep. He'd had a heart attack and was unable to continue his job for now. John had been sworn in as president right outside William's hospital room. One camera crew was chosen from the news media pool to cover it live. They were all trying to get more information about William's condition. Following the brief ceremony John held a news conference. He told the world that President Noble had suffered a major heart attack and was very ill. Then, he couldn't help himself, he asked the country to pray for William. John knew he had just crossed a line, but he didn't care. If God could help William, John wanted Him to. He wanted to be president but not this way. He wanted William back on his feet, and the sooner the better.

The morning newspapers featured the headline, "President Ill and Vice President Turns to God." The phone didn't stop ringing for the rest of the week.

Milton Borsch was fit to be tied. He quickly decided he would have to do something, and do it fast. The vice president obviously was not a good choice for the country. All his plans were based around William and the Liberal Party. He had been working on this for years, using every crisis to chip away at Christian freedoms and nobody was going to get in his way now.

Dan and Jeff had both received anonymous phone calls with tips about the murders they were investigating. Dan had heard the name many times. He knew Milton Borsch was a progressive far left member of and supporter of the Liberal Party. Rumor was he had invested many millions of dollars into their campaigns. His AFA was actually doing great harm to our freedoms. He was considered radical by some. The caller had informed them that he was behind several murders including Beverly Davis and Laura Johnson. Maybe it was time to have a talk with Mr. James Carson their number one suspect. They might be able to link the two murders together. It was worth a try. The two reporters started their investigation right away. They were sharing information with the police captain and a task force from the FBI

CHAPTER TWENTY THREE

Car Bombed

F redrick was heading to the office early. He kissed little Rebecca goodbye and told Diane he would see her for lunch. They were meeting at The White House later for lunch with her father. She walked him to the door and watched as he got into his car. When he started his car the bomb detonated instantly. She felt the heat of the blast as the front door knocked her off her feet. Diane was dazed but quickly recovered and came running from the house as several neighbors were approaching what was left of Fredrick's car. Her screams could be heard from blocks away. She was inconsolable.

The phone rang in the oval office. John Paul was summoned to his daughter's side. She was overcome with grief.

"Daddy why?" she cried. "Fredrick never hurt anyone. He was always helping people. Who would want him dead? Oh Daddy please help me." Her cries were as pathetic as a small child's. Diane was overcome with grief.

Rebecca came in right behind John. She had called Diane's doctor. He was on his way. She felt sure he would sedate the young mother. Rebecca would care for the baby. J.P. and Jillian had also been called. They would be there soon. The Feds were asking questions and the media was outraged.

Dan called Luke and told him the news. Luke immediately called the airport to book a flight to Washington. His friends were under attack. One was dead and the other was in grief and shock. Luke knew how Diane felt and he knew she would need help. He brushed away the tears that started rolling down his face. He went into his bedroom and prayed his heart out.

The news was full of the death of Fredrick Shells. He was, after all the Son-in-Law of the Vice President, and now Acting President of The United States Of America. William's heart attack was front page news and so was Fredrick's death. They were reporting that John Paul Cavender had all that he could handle.

Diane was taken to the hospital. She was in such a state of shock that no one could get through to her. Rebecca took the baby home with her. The Secret Service were stationed outside her hospital room. They were there to protect her as well as John. No one knew why her husband had been killed, and as far as they knew she could also be a target. John sat quietly at her bedside. He knew she was sedated of course, but he just couldn't leave her now. The Secret Service knocked on her door and told John that someone named Luke Davis was here to see Diane. John told them to let him in. Luke shook hands with John and expressed his sorrow for his family. John had never looked into kinder eyes than this man's. He walked over to Diane's bed and bowed his head and prayed for her. John had never experienced anything like that prayer. It was electrifying. After Luke finished praying he asked John if there was anything he could do to help him and his family.

"Just keep praying son." John whispered.

"I will," Luke promised as he reached out and touched John's shoulder in an expression of concern.

John felt the tears start. He sobbed and cried for his beautiful daughter and Fredrick. He cried for his mother and his country. He must have cried for fifteen minutes before he could compose himself again. As he brushed away his tears he saw that Luke was crying with him. Luke's compassion almost moved John to tears again. John somehow knew in that moment that God was in the room. For the first time in his life he believed that God loved him. He also understood that God was real. He could feel His presence. He thought about his mother's prayers. She had prayed for him so many times. He always just tried to ignore her. That was when he was young and confused. Now he was thankful that Luke was there and that he was praying for them.

Luke offered to sit with Diane and let John go get some rest.

It took some insisting but he finally agreed to go for a while. He told Luke that he would return with Rebecca as soon as he freshened up and grabbed a sandwich.

"Take as much time as you need," Luke told him.

Diane moaned a little then she started crying. Luke went over to her bedside to console her as the nurse prepared an injection. Luke whispered the twenty third psalms to her and she quieted down. For the next few days he sat with her constantly repeating scriptures and assuring her he wouldn't leave. He knew how badly she needed a Christian friend right now. Her parents and brother kept a close watch over her, but it seemed that Luke was the one who could help her the most. He constantly reminded her that she was in the presence of the Lord and He would not forsake her.

Rebecca wiped tears every time she came into the room. She was drawn to Luke's voice as he comforted her daughter. She realized that he was a comfort to all of them.

J.P. stood quietly at his sister's bedside. He was terribly worried. He wondered if his family would be next. He thanked Luke over and over for coming to help with Diane. He knew about Beverly so he understood that Luke shared her grief in a way he couldn't.

"I didn't realize how dangerous these people were." He spoke quietly almost to himself. He remembered the day he said he didn't care if he never heard from another Christian, right now he'd give anything to hear Fredrick speak to him about Jesus again. He feared

Diane would never be the same. She had seen her husband blown to bits. What if it had been Jillian, or God forbid Alex or Adeline? What would he do?

Luke's voice broke into his train of thought. He was telling Rebecca he would be staying until after the memorial service. He assured them he would be honored to speak for Fredrick. He related stories from school. He told them how they met.

"We were headed in the same direction. I wasn't paying a lot of attention to my surroundings. Just as I stepped off the curb a car come barreling around the corner. I could have been killed that day, but Fredrick grabbed me and pulled me to safety. After that I owed him my life. Our friendship began that day. We have always been pretty close, but we each had different goals."

He told them how Fredrick tried to protect Diane's identity. "He loved her more than life," Luke told them. "Right after Beverly died, Fredrick called me. He said that he had received a threatening phone call. He said he feared his life was in danger. He was most concerned for his wife and daughter. He was the bravest man I've ever known. He was a powerhouse in the Lords Army, just as my Beverly was. We can't bring them back, as much as we'd like to, but we have the promise that we can meet them again someday in God's beautiful heaven." The family seemed to feel better under the calming effect of his voice. It was caring and sincere.

Finally Diane started responding to their voices. Luke spoke to her in gentle tones. She cried as she asked about her baby. They told her that baby Rebecca was fine, just missing her mommy. Then she asked Luke if Fredrick was alright. He promised her that Fredrick was safe in the arms of Jesus. "Beverly will look out for him he whispered in a choked voice." John and Rebecca realized how hard this must be for him, yet he never complained or offered to leave her side. He truly was a man of God.

The next morning Diane announced that she wanted to go home. She said "My baby needs me and I need to take care of the arrangements for Fredrick's service."

Luke asked if she would like for him to take her home, so John and Rebecca could pick up the baby for her. She thanked him and said yes. She was quiet on the way home and as they neared the spot where Fredrick died she started to cry.

Luke patted her hand and said, "Remember he's in the arms of Jesus now."

After that day Diane seemed to have control over her emotions. She prayed constantly for strength and soon she hoped to go back to work. Diane didn't know how she would cope with living in the home she and Fredrick had made together. Everywhere she looked there were reminders of the life they had shared.

"Jesus," she prayed, "I know he is safe with you. Help me to do your will without him. Right now I don't know how to do that, but I am sure you will lead me."

CHAPTER TWENTY FOUR

A Funeral

John Paul was busy running the White House as William recovered. When the phone in the Oval Office rang that morning, John answered but didn't recognize the voice. He started to hang up when the voice sneered at him.

"The next time we will get her too." John felt his blood running cold.

"Who are you?" He demanded.

"Ask your Dear President who I am. If he gets out of the hospital he had better be signing a bill into law fast and you Mr. Vice President need to know that no one is safe until these religious fanatics are put out of business."

John Paul left for the hospital right away. William had some questions to answer. If he knew who was threatening his family and killing people he had better tell him. His daughter was just threatened again and his Son-in-Law was dead. He wanted answers now.

Steve was just coming to work as John came out of The Oval Office.

"What is wrong sir?" He asked John.

"I am so angry," John said. "Someone is killing my family and I think William knows who it is."

Steve wondered how much John knew about Milton Borsch.

"John let's go have a talk with William. I will find out for you, and I will help you. It's not right for these murderers to get away with this even if they are filthy rich. No one should be bought and paid for like this."

John didn't have a clue what Steve was talking about, but he had a feeling he was getting ready to find out. There must be more to this than he even expected.

William was feeling much better when they walked into the room, but one look at John's face told him all was not well. "I'll be leaving here today." He told them in a cheerful voice.

"That's great Sir," Steve responded.

John didn't waste any time with small talk he got right to the point. "William I received a phone call today. The person on the other end told me he had killed Fredrick and that Diane would be next. When I asked who he was, he said to ask you. William I want some answers and I want them now." William knew exactly who had called but he was trying to decide how to handle this when John's rising voice interrupted his thoughts. "You tell me right now or so help me I will go to the press, the FBI, or anyone else that will listen. There are too many innocent people dying. One of them was even my son-in-law. I'd advise you to start talking."

William took a deep breath and said one name. "Milton Borsch, he called me the night I had my heart attack. John, he is crazy. He's threatening all of us if this bill isn't passed and made law."

"William why didn't you tell me?" John implored. "He is killing my family and I don't even know why."

"He's a fanatic John and he's an atheist. He told me he has been working on this bill for years. He further stated that he had put us all in office and he would take us all out if this bill didn't become law. He said you were not on our team. John I would have told you, but I had my heart attack before I could get to you."

"That's the truth sir" Steve spoke up. "We are working on this and the Feds are involved, and so is the media. We are all working together undercover."

It made sense to John. Fredrick was killed right after William had the heart attack.

"I swear to you John until that night I had no idea who was having people killed." William promised.

"What are we going to do?" John asked.

"John we really need you to act as though you know nothing. Keep your family under guard twenty four hours a day."

"Don't worry, I will and I want to be kept in the loop at all times. When is this bill going to be passed anyway?"

"Soon, William told him, very soon. Then we should all be safe. I will sign it as soon as it comes up from The Hill. I don't want any more bloodshed over this."

John felt totally disgusted. This man he had always respected so much was a bought and paid for coward. However he didn't know any other way to keep his family safe than to give them what they wanted. Maybe they could overturn The Law later. Then John thought of Luke. He was kind and brave and he is still fighting on although his wife was murdered. Diane would not change her mind either. Some of these Christians are really committed. At least you could respect them. They stood for what they believed in even as they faced death. John decided he would resume his Bible reading tonight. Maybe he would ask Luke some questions. He really did need answers. Who was this Man called Jesus, that His people would die for Him? He knew without a doubt that only death would stop Luke, yet the young man had never put him down for his job. He has always just treated me with concern, John thought as tears rolled down his face again.

William was back in the oval office the next day. He had been cleared by his doctors and the transfer of power back to William was handled with much less fanfare than when John was sworn in. Nobody was any happier about William being back than John. He was still worried about William, he looked a little pale, but he told John he would rest in the afternoon. William told John to take off a few days to be with his family.

John knew William was sorry for his loss. William wasn't a bad person, just a power hungry coward.

Fredrick's Memorial service was scheduled for the next morning. Luke prayed for guidance as he prepared the eulogy he would give. He hoped he could encourage Diane and her family. He knew John was having a really hard time. He felt guilty, because his job was putting them all in danger. Luke liked John. He believed he was a good man, just confused about religion. He wasn't the only one. Half the country seemed to oppose Christianity. There were few times in history the country had been so divided. The liberals had touted diversity and tolerance even verging on the ridiculous, yet somehow anything and everything, except Christianity, was included. Luke knew he would never stop serving God no matter what was done to him. He also realized that God would take care of him. He was not afraid, just determined to do his Father's will.

The large church was packed with members, family and invited guests. The Secret Service could be seen everywhere. Luke spoke in a gentle voice as he told about his friend. Sometimes they laughed at their antics as Luke told them about their college days.

"I always thought that Fredrick would be a minister. Even in school he had a deep faith in God. Next to him I felt like a sinner." Then Luke's voice filled with tears.

"He was my friend. One of the first who offered to help me on this journey. He didn't die in vain. He's a martyr for the cause of Christ and he is safe in Heaven now. We can't bring him back, but we can go to be with him." Luke felt the sweet touch of Jesus as he spoke these final words.

"In closing I want to leave you with these words from the Bible. I have set before you, life and death, blessing and cursing: therefore choose life that both thou and thy seed may live. Fredrick choose life and now he lives forevermore. Let us pray."

CHAPTER TWENTY FIVE

Moving On

Diane wandered around the house for a few weeks. She knew she needed to be busy, but she couldn't make herself go back to work. Finally she decided to set up an office in Nashville so she would be closer to the work that she and Fredrick were committed to. She couldn't bear to stay in their house in Washington any longer. It was a constant reminder of his horrible death. She wished she could work at this full time now. She knew that was not possible, but she would not allow Fredrick's death to be in vain, or Beverly's either. Diane heard, through her father, that the vote was being held up again. She also heard that there would soon be an arrest in Fredrick's murder. Diane knew no fear as she went forward. What could they do to her? They had already taken away the person she loved the most in the world. They could take her life, but they couldn't take her soul. It belonged to God. If they did kill her she would just go to be with Fredrick and her sweet Jesus in heaven.

Dan and Jeff had arranged to sit in on a meeting between the Feds and James Carson. They couldn't ask any questions directly, but they could write down questions and the Feds would ask them. James was a quiet man. His blonde hair was natural and his piercing blue eyes had no feeling in them at all. He seemed totally void of emotion as he listened to the Feds. They hinted about offering a deal if he told them what they wanted. They wanted to know about a man named Milton Borsch. His name kept popping up in murders that they believed James had committed.

James wasn't talking yet. He was being held without bond and so far no deal had actually been offered. None that would make him talk anyway. He knew how to play the game. The more desperate they became the better the offer. He told them all where they could go, and called for the corrections officer to take him back to his cell.

"He's got the goods on Milton but he's waiting for a plea bargain." Dan said.

The Feds were in no hurry to give him one. They would let him sweat it out for a while and then tell him they were going to offer Milton a plea to testify against him. Of course he would spill his guts then, especially if they offered to take the death penalty off the table.

Luke sat in Diane's office looking over the lawsuit she was planning to file. He knew she was a fighter and he was proud of her, but he did feel concern for her relationship with her father. Diane assured him that she and her dad would be fine.

"We have an understanding." She said and smiled.

Luke couldn't help but notice how pale she still looked. She had dark circles under her eyes. As usual, her eyes were red rimmed from crying. Even in her grieving she was still very beautiful. She was gracious and kind. She had taken Fredrick's death very hard as he had Beverly's. Now they were both determined to go on with the fight to save Christian freedoms.

"What do you say we go have some lunch?" Luke said,

"You can fill me in on the legal matters you are involved in."

Diane agreed and soon they were seated in a small diner having sandwiches. Luke continued his thoughts from before,

"Diane I can't tell you how thankful I am for your dedication."

"Luke, When Fredrick first died I didn't think I could go on. I wanted to die too. Even the baby couldn't comfort me, but every time I think of what our own government is trying to do to us I get indignant. Then I want to live and fight until we win or until Jesus takes me home." Diane said with as much determination and energy as Luke had ever seen from her.

"I know what you mean." Luke replied, "I didn't think that I could go on for a while after Beverly died either. Then I realized that she died for this very cause. She would never have given in to fear, and I won't either."

CHAPTER TWENTY SIX

Milton Arrested

"The vote has been rescheduled again." John told Diane. "I think the exposure of Milton Borsch has scared the Senate. He financed most of their campaigns. They're scared now that their names will be linked to his. They don't want to give the Christian's more ammunition to fight them with. They know the press will have a field day with this information."

When the Speaker of the House first heard that Milton was picked up for questioning, he called his friend Charles, the Senator from New York. He wanted to let him know that there was trouble in the air. "What is going on with Milton?" David Forman asked. "I hear he is losing it. He is openly threatening the Vice President's Daughter and it was recorded."

"He also said he knew about her husband's death. How crazy is that?" Charles asked.

The House Speaker was very upset. "We all owe our jobs to him. He sure gave us millions for our campaigns. I don't know what is possessing him now. If he keeps talking this crazy stuff he could bring us all down. Do you know if he had anything to do with that nastiness in New York? You know, the murder of Laura Johnson."

"I don't know anything about that David," Charles's replied, so David continued.

"It seems he hired her to get the pastor off our backs. Then she was found dead right after he paid her off. They never recovered the money. Someone shot her and took the money. I hear he had a man named Carson on the payroll. He is a professional hit man. I'm sorry I ever took his money, but I couldn't have won without it." David confessed.

"Me either," Charles said, "But I haven't heard a word from him since the New York Primary. He called to congratulate me."

"Well I heard he had plenty to say to William. That's what caused his heart attack. He told me he was considering stepping down as president due to his health, but I think he's just running scared right now."

"If Milton is mixed up in murder then we all need to be afraid. This could ruin us." David and Charles decided to talk later, after they found out what some of the other Representatives were thinking.

The FBI picked up Milton Borsch for questioning. He lawyered up immediately, so they arrested him on various charges including conspiracy to murder. He wouldn't say a word, so after arraignment he posted a large bond and went home. His lawyer asked to see the evidence against him. The Feds told them they would send over a copy of the tape of him threatening the Vice President's Daughter and taking responsibility for her husband's death. They told him that was only the beginning. James Carson is about ready to spill his guts and when he does we will link your client to at least two more murders.

Bob Harris thought it sounded like his client's past was about to catch up with him and decided to try a new tactic. He let it be known that his client was a man of great means who would be very generous to anyone who made these charges go away. He was surprised at how quickly the agent let him know he was in danger of sharing a cell with his client if he continued to talk that way.

Bob Harris left the FBI office and went straight to see his client. Milton was a mess. "Who do they think they are?" He asked his lawyer, "Don't they know I've got more money and power than God?"

"Listen Milton, I'm just your lawyer but if I were you I'd be keeping a very low profile. It seems they've got the goods on you. They say it is all on tape." Bob Harris said.

"They have nothing," Milton hissed back at him. "They are just fishing that's all."

"I will try to help you, but I think I should warn you these Feds can't be bought off like the locals you have in your pocket. I know you've been doing that all your life, but it won't work with these guys."

"Everybody has got a price. You just have to find out what it is. Just ask our esteemed president. I own him and he can make all of this disappear with a phone call."

"Not this time, you've threatened to kill the Vice President's Daughter."

"I will too, if they don't get these charges dropped."

Bob never did like this client, and right now he almost hated him. Milton was so sure that he could do anything he pleased and get away with it. Sadly, he had gotten away with a lot, including murder, simply with intimidation and paying people off. Bob had twisted a few arms for him also. Bob would like to quit representing him, but he owed him too much, and Milton could implicate him for the dirty tricks he had done for him. He probably wouldn't go to jail for any of them but he could certainly loose his license to practice law. Like everyone else he was bought and paid for. Murder charges, however weren't likely to go away, unless they could put it on someone else. That was definitely a possibility they had done that before too.

CHAPTER TWENTY SEVEN

✳

The Feds Have the Goods

Diane was looking for a house to buy. She was selling the one she owned in Washington. She didn't want anything too extravagant. She would need something big enough for her nanny to have her own quarters. She also wanted office space, and plenty of room to entertain. She knew as the new girl in town she would have to make connections so she could make a living. She also wanted plenty of time to devote to the federal lawsuit. Nothing could come before that. She had wanted to do this full time, but then her better judgment took over and she knew she wanted to earn a living for herself and baby Rebecca. Fredrick had left them very well off with insurance and savings, but she wanted to know she was making a contribution too. As she talked to one realtor after another it seemed she just couldn't find what she needed. Eventually she decided to have a house custom built for her. She called Luke to see if he could recommend someone to build her a house. He told her he would get some information together for her. She told him she was going to visit her parents for a few days and asked if he would mind watering her plants while she was gone.

He said, I'll drop by your office tomorrow morning and get a key."

"Thanks Luke I couldn't make it without you."

"I'm sure you could but I'm always glad to give you a hand. By the way have you eaten yet?"

"Not yet, I hate eating alone."

"Me too. I'll pick you up in an hour."

"I'll be ready," She almost cried as she thought of the two of them trying so hard to get along without their spouses.

"I'm so lonely," she later confided in Luke. "If it wasn't for my work and my baby I don't know what I would do. You have been such a good friend to me."

"We've been good friends to each other," he said.

William called John into his office. "I may have to resign from office," he said. "I don't want to but my health is failing, and of course you know I have Milton to contend with. He is going to ruin us all I'm afraid."

"He is not going to ruin me," John responded. "I've never taken a dime from him. Even if I had I wouldn't feel like I had to resign. He's the one who is murdering people not you or me."

"I guess I never thought of it like that. I certainly don't agree with what he is doing. I guess I'm afraid of guilt by association. He is completely crazy. He's demanding that we all either pass the bill or resign. He is saying we owe it to him."

"The Feds will take care of him I'm sure," John assured William. "I have heard through the grapevine that they are building quite a case against him now. They are tying him to a hit man named Carson that has been killing Christians and anyone else Milton tells him to. They have financial records that they say can prove that Milton has him on his payroll. Milton's lawyer is trying to make a deal for him, but Milton won't deal. They could go with insanity, but Milton won't do that either. I guess he really thinks his money will free him. I know he had Fredrick killed and Diane could still be in danger."

"John, I cannot tell you how sorry I am for all of this. I would have called you that night, but my chest started hurting and the next thing I knew I was in the hospital and you were there with me. Milton really carried on badly. I finally called Steve in and told him to handle it. Believe me it's being taken care of."

Diane arrived in Washington early Saturday morning. Rebecca ran to greet her and was surprised at how well she looked.

"I am selling my house here in Washington," she told her family. "I want to move everything to Nashville. I am getting ready to build a house there. I wondered if baby Rebecca could stay on with you, Mom, until I'm better situated. I want her to have stability and right now there is not a lot of that in my life."

"Of course she can stay here with us for as long as you need her to. We love having her."

The baby smiled up at her mom as if to say, it will be alright Mom. I understand. She was so precious. She kept them all smiling. Diane was overwhelmed with their love. She brought them all up to date on what was happening with her law practice.

John told her once again how much he liked and respected Luke.

"He sure loves you and he loved Fredrick too," he observed. "He never left your side in the hospital except to take a shower and change clothes. He prayed for you constantly and I was impressed. He put his own grief aside and grieved with us. I guess that's just another reason why Christians are so special."

"Daddy he reminds me of Grandmother Cavender. He has that same loving quality about him, just like Fredrick did. Grandmother was special. She taught me to love Jesus. I will always be thankful to her for that."

"She was a good woman," John said, as he was reminded of all the times she had tried to talk to him.

The Senators were having many closed door sessions. They were trying to decide how to go on with the vote now that Milton was in so much trouble.

"We have put it off long enough," David Forman said. "We should have taken care of this months ago instead we are all dragging our feet. I suggest we set a new date and this time and move forward on the bill."

David was a third generation Atheist. His parents and their parents were all God deniers. He hated being preached to all the time. He wanted his rights protected. He wasn't about to give up the fight. Milton may be out of the battle but there was plenty of big money around and he knew where it was.

Luke got a call from Dan that morning. He asked if they could meet. Luke invited him over and Dan wasted no time getting there. He was very excited. He thanked Luke for agreeing to meet right away. Things were getting ready to blow wide open. Their investigation had uncovered all kinds of corruption in the Liberal Party.

"We now know who killed Laura Johnson and why. We also know who was behind Beverly's and Fredrick's murders. The Feds are just about ready to start bringing people to justice and you will never believe who put us onto these creeps. This is top secret but the vice president of this country took a stand and he turned Milton in. Seems he has so much money he was trying to buy the Liberal Party, but John wasn't indebted to him in any way. He blew the whistle loud and clear. He's a good man. The rest was just plain old hard detective work. But we've got them all."

Luke was rejoicing at every word. "I knew my God would bring it all out into the open. My sweet wife loved Him above everything and I knew He wouldn't fail her. Dan, I am so thankful to you and all who are working with you on this. You will never know what this means to me."

Dan wiped his eyes and tried to compose himself, but he realized this man standing before him was the real deal. He was a Christian through and through. "Pray for me Luke," He said in a choked voice. "I want to know your Jesus."

Luke explained the plan of salvation to Dan in a language a child could understand. (Romans 3:23 KJV) "For all have sinned and come short of the glory of God." (Romans 6:23a KJV) "For the wages of sin is death." (Romans 5; 8-9 KJV) "But God commendeth his love toward us, in that, while we were yet sinners, Christ died for us. Much more then, being now justified by his blood, we shall be saved from wrath through him" (Romans 10: 9-10,13 KJV) "That if though shalt confess with thy mouth the Lord Jesus, and shall believe in thine heart that God hath raised him from the dead, though shalt be saved. For with the heart man believeth unto righteousness, and with the mouth confession is made unto righteousness. For whosoever shall call upon the name of the Lord shall be saved"

Then they both knelt down and prayed for God to reveal himself to Dan. "Save his soul Lord and give him eternal life in you." Luke prayed earnestly for his friend. He knew God had sent Dan to him and he thanked him.

Dan knew Jesus at last. He told Luke that he was in for the duration of the battle. They hugged each other and praised the Lord. Dan couldn't wait to tell Jeff. He knew that Jeff needed a Savior too.

It seemed Luke could hear Beverly singing, "I'm in the Lord's Army. I'm in the Lord's Army." She surely must be looking down on me from heaven, he thought.

After that day Luke didn't feel so lonely anymore. He knew she was with him in Spirit. He must remember to tell Diane about his experience. He knew how lonely she was too. He wished she were back from Washington so he could ask her to have lunch with him. He wanted to tell her what God was doing through Dan. Just about that time the phone rang. It was Diane.

"I was thinking about lunch, she said. Do you want to go?"

"Praise God," he whispered, "I'd love too.

It was now almost six months since Beverly's death and there had been many changes in Luke's life. The new church building was complete and their home had been rebuilt. The boys still spent most of their time with their grandparent's, but visited him on weekends. They were doing quite well thanks to all the people who surrounded them with love. Diane's move to Nashville had helped him tremendously and her new house would be ready in early fall. The Senators in Washington were still trying to have a vote and God's people were on fire. Milton was going to be tried in Federal Court for the murders of Laura Johnson, Beverly and Fredrick, and John was pushing for the death penalty. James Carson was going to testify against Milton to keep from getting the death penalty himself. They had even been able to identify the bomber. A guy named Ben Harmon was going to testify that Milton had paid him to plant bombs in Luke's home and church. He was also the one who had bombed Fredrick's car.

Milton still believed he would pay somebody off, and get out of all these charges. This time however, he was dealing with the power of Almighty God and Milton, in spite of his bragging otherwise, did not have more power than God.

Luke still missed Beverly, but now his unbearable pain, was being replaced with more beautiful thoughts and memories of her. He visited her grave every few weeks and brought her fresh flowers. He told her everything that was going on. He knew she wasn't there. She was in heaven. He somehow believed that she knew he was alright.

CHAPTER TWENTY EIGHT

The Vote Scheduled

Word finally came to the president that the vote had been scheduled. He told John right away. That is when John told him he was taking his family on a cruise and would see him in a few weeks. The president wished he were going too. This had been too much for him. He would sign their stupid bill into law and be done with it.

Diane really hated to go knowing Fredrick would have been there if he hadn't been killed, still she didn't want to disappoint her mom and dad. She also wanted to spend some quality time with Baby Rebecca. Finally, she admitted to herself that she really didn't want to leave Luke.

"Oh Lord, am I falling in love with him or what? Fredrick hasn't been gone a year and I'm constantly thinking about Luke. Please forgive me. I love Fredrick but Lord I'm so lonely." The tears started falling and she cried like she hadn't since Fredrick first died. Great swells of emotion rocked her body. Afterwards she felt completely at peace. She would leave this in God's hands.

That night John called Luke and invited him on the cruise. John explained that he knew his family needed a rest before the trial started and he wondered if Luke might not need a break too.

Luke thanked him for the invitation and told him he would see about clearing his calendar. He promised to call him back the next day.

John didn't know why, but he really wanted Luke to come with them. He almost seemed like part of the family. They didn't see eye to eye on some things, but he still liked Luke a lot. He had certainly been a life saver for Diane. John could never repay him for that. He told Rebecca and she thought it was a good idea too. When J.P. called, he told him and Jillian his plan and they both agreed it would be good to have Luke join them.

"Maybe he can explain his faith to us" Jillian said. "I'd sure like to know more about it. He has peace like I've never seen before, and I long for that peace myself."

When Luke informed Diane that he had been invited on their family cruise, she was more than a little pleased.

He said, "I don't want to intrude, but your family is the closest thing to family I've ever had. Beverly's parents are wonderful folks. They always treated me good of course. Now I feel like an outsider again since she's gone. It's not their fault. We just all loved her so much that now we are constant reminders to each other that we will never have her again here on this earth. However, they are wonderful with the children and my kids need that family atmosphere that they provide. I am very grateful to them. My parents were killed when I was three years old, so I never knew them. I was raised by my grandmother and she passed away while I was still in college. I have no brothers or sisters. I have my heavenly Father and my wonderful Savior. They have seen me through my whole life and I know they will never leave me."

Diane once again was impressed by this wonderful friend of hers. She was so glad that Fredrick had introduced them.

"I will be happy to share my family with you," she said. Now she was looking forward to the cruise. She wouldn't feel so alone.

The big ship sat in the Miami Harbor. Luke looked quite handsome in his polo shirt and a pair of khaki shorts. Diane was dressed in white shorts and a pink top. The family had just given their luggage to the purser and they were ready to board the ship. Luke gave him his suitcase as well and they headed up the gangplank. A few weeks in the sunshine would be great for them all. The Bahamas was a favorite vacation spot for the Cavender Family. Luke was impressed with the size of the ship. The cabins were spacious and beautifully decorated. As Luke dressed for dinner he thought of Beverly and wished she could be here with him. It wasn't unusual for him to wear a suit but not necessarily for dinner. They were traveling first class all the way. They had been invited to dine at the Captain's Table. Luke had never seen such grandeur as this. Everything was big and magnificent and it all seemed to sparkle. Music played throughout the large ship. It was so peaceful. There were constantly many things to do, however he preferred to just visit with the family.

On their first night Jillian asked Luke if he would share his faith with them. Luke had been praying for the opportunity to do just that. It became a nightly appointment for them to gather and Luke would teach them from the Bible. They were starving for the word of God. He explained the birth, death and resurrection of Jesus. He told them that The Lamb of God was sacrificed for them. He helped them to understand why it was so important that Christians have the freedom to introduce others to Jesus. He explained that each person had to choose for themselves who they would serve. He told them about the beauty of Heaven and the horror of Hell. He didn't mince words. He just told them the truth. He knew that they were searching. All he could do was teach them and pray.

Diane was so much help. She was a faithful Christian, but she never preached to her family. She just lived her Christian life before them, and prayed that one day they too would accept Jesus as she

97

had when she was just a little girl. Grandmother Cavender would be so happy to know that at last her son was listening to the Word of God.

The sunshine and the sea breeze of the beautiful island seemed to agree with them all. It had a healing effect. Alex and Adeline were enjoying the water, swimming and surfing. Everyone was in good spirits when the call came in that John needed to fly back to Washington as soon as possible. The vote had been taken. They were hopelessly tied. It was as they expected, split right down party lines. John would have to cast the final vote, the tiebreaker.

Diane started to cry. "Daddy I know you have to do what you feel is right and so do I, but I will always love you no matter how you vote."

Luke prayed for John all that night. He knew Diane's heart was broken and so was his. He prayed that God would somehow show John the right way. After almost two weeks of Bible study and prayer Luke felt he had done just about all he could do. He had to put John in the hands of God.

John felt a little sad when he lay down that night. He finally drifted into a troubled sleep. Then he started to dream. It started with John in Washington. He was casting the tiebreaking vote. The final vote had been made now it was up to William. With his vote the bill had passed the senate. John was relieved to have it over with. He knew Diane wouldn't agree with his vote, but after all he owed his loyalty to his party. He decided he would not discuss it again with anyone. He had done what was expected of him. In return for his vote, the big money would help him get elected president. That was all he cared about. Then John left the White House to go on vacation.

Suddenly John found himself standing on the top of a beautiful mountain. There was a summer breeze in the air. The entire family was there having a picnic. The birds were singing their pretty songs, and everything was so peaceful. John had never felt such peace. Then the earth exploded into sound. At first it sounded like a great trumpet. Then he heard the roar of loud booming thunder. Suddenly the clouds opened up and rolled back as a scroll, and he heard music. It was so beautiful and inviting. It seemed to saturate his whole being. John felt as though he could melt right into the music. Then he looked up and saw angels floating above him. John couldn't believe his eyes. There was his mother, standing in a cloud reaching out to him. She looked so beautiful and happy. John remembered when she had told him that Jesus would come like a thief in the night. It paid to be ready.

As he held baby Rebecca a force much greater than he was tore her from his arms. Then he saw Jesus, in all His glory and majesty and he knew Him because he saw the nail scars in his hands and feet. He remembered the times that his mother had told him of a place called Calvary. She said that he was nailed to a cross where he paid for their sins. That he still bore the nail scars in his hands and feet. She had begged John to accept Jesus as his Savior. His arms were outstretched to Baby Rebecca as she started floating up to Jesus. Oh what a pretty sight she was laughing and holding her arms out to Him as though she had just been waiting for Him to come. That's silly he thought she's just a baby. As Jesus took her in his arms he saw two more babies floating right up to baby Rebecca. John knew they were the little ones that Diane had lost to miscarriage. Next he saw his beloved Daughter Diane floating right up to join her babies. Fredrick was standing next to Jesus with the most beautiful smile he had ever seen welcoming them to Heaven. "Oh Diane, I'm so sorry," John cried. "I should have listened to you and Fredrick and Mother. You were right and I was wrong." John started to run away. He hoped the rocks and the mountains would cover him up. He had never imagined a day like this. Stunned, he couldn't move. He felt as though his feet were cast in cement. He couldn't run. In the next instant the ground started rumbling under his feet. He could feel it moving like a great earthquake, tossing him into the air and then back down again. By now John was crying and begging for help. Then he felt the ground open up and there were screams coming from the belly of the earth. Then he saw him, a great dragon, that old serpent called the Devil. Satan, who deceived the whole world.

Satan said to John, "Why hello there my faithful servant. You know who I am?" John's fear was so bad that he was trembling. He knew exactly who he was.

John said, "I have never been your servant. I am The Vice President of the United States of America. I have great power you know."

Satan just laughed at him, "You have no power over me. The only one who has ever had power over me is Jesus Christ, the Son of God, and you rejected Him."

John asked "What do you know about the Bible?"

Satin replied, "If you would have read The Word, you would know I'm in The Bible. My works are all through The Bible. I know it better than you do.

As he spoke smoke gushed from his mouth and nostrils. The smell was overpowering. John could smell the very fire and brimstone. Satan's eyes were glowing as dark coals of brimstone and John knew he was in the presence of evil.

Satan said, "All I ever had to do was feed your pride. I know, you're the vice president, and you think that makes you special. I've been deceiving you for years." He laughed a terrible laugh and continued. "While you were caught up in your accomplishments. God called you, and you had the power to vote down that bill, but you wanted to be president. So now you have the blood of many on your hands. Oh you fool," He laughed again, a horrible hollow sound of glee, and his piercing red eyes seemed to look right through John as he said, "I win! You belong to me now, and so do they."

John stood helplessly by as his beloved Rebecca was swallowed up. The look on her face accusing him. Screaming for John to help her. J.P. was crying and begging his father to stop this madness. Then he heard the screams of Alex and Adeline. John fell to his knees and started pleading with God to save them.

God asked him, "Why are you calling on me? I don't know you."

John tried to explain that his mother had prayed many prayers for him. "Surely you know my mother. She loved you more than anything. Her name is Sara Cavender."

"Yes, I do, her name is right here in The Lamb's Book of Life. She accepted my Son Jesus as her personal Savior many years ago, but you never did. She tried to warn you that I would come again and you needed to be ready. According to my record you politely ignored her pleas."

But I thought about it, I don't know why I didn't. I was young and dumb I guess. Maybe I'd planned on doing it when I was older. I didn't expect you to come when you did. Please give me another chance and I'll serve you faithfully."

"It's too late now Son. Time is up." God told him, "How many times did you turn my Son away? He knocked and knocked at the door of your heart. You never let him in. You even tried to abolish my word from the very earth that I created. Why should I help you?"

As guilt washed over John he knew God was right, He didn't know him. John had never acknowledged Jesus as his Savior. The blood had never cleansed his soul. He wouldn't let Jesus in. He had had many opportunities, John knew it was all true.

Finally he bowed his head and said, "You shouldn't help me. I deserve to die and go to hell. But please help my family. My daughter is in Heaven. She prayed for me and the rest of her family."

"Yes she did, faithfully, and I heard her prayers. Do you remember the sleepless nights when you felt afraid? I was there all the time pleading with you to trust me. I wanted to set you free of fear. I loved you, but you always turned a deaf ear to me. I tried to persuade you to take your family to church. They would have gone with you. They trusted you. You knew the truth through your mother, but you never did accept it for yourself. Now their blood is on your hands along with many others. You could have made a difference not just for your family but an entire nation, but you chose power and prestige over your very soul. You watched as they were destroying my churches, you did nothing to save them. So why are you calling on me now?"

Then John saw a look of pure love mixed with pain in the eyes of God, as he said "Time has run out for you. The blood of my Son has never been applied to your soul, Depart from me ye worker of iniquity. I never knew you."

With that John felt himself falling into a bottomless pit called hell. He realized the sound he was hearing was his own screaming. He also realized that he could hear the screams and the gnashing of teeth of others. If only he had another chance. He would give anything in exchange for his soul.

"John, wake up" it was Rebecca.

"What's wrong sweetheart?" He asked.

His tortured cries had awakened her. John was burning up with fever. He was chilling so bad he was shaking the bed. Rebecca couldn't make out what he was saying, something about Satan. Tears were flowing down his face and he was sobbing uncontrollably.

"I'm going to get the ship's doctor." she cried.

"Rebecca, I don't need a doctor." He said in a tortured voice. "Go get Luke," he cried, "I need a preacher. We must give our hearts to Jesus right now."

"John what are you talking about?" She believed he must be out of his head with fever. Never, in all the years she had known him, had he ever acted like he was now. Rebecca felt afraid for him. Was he losing it or having a heart attack? She didn't know what was possessing him.

The dream had been so real to John that it took him a long time to get his bearings and clear his head enough to be understood.

Then he told her about the dream. He still shivered and cried as he related it to her. She knew he was telling her the truth when he said, "Rebecca it was God warning me."

"I'll go get Luke" she said.

"Ask all the family to come in here please. I must warn them."

She could hear the desperation in his voice. He was pleading with her to hurry. She went to wake the rest of the family.

CHAPTER TWENTY NINE

The Dream

After the family gathered in the room, John told them about the dream. He told Diane how happy Fredrick was.

"Your Grandmother and another pretty lady are taking good care of him." John wept as he told her that he had seen her little babies that she had miscarried. They are right there with Jesus. By then they were all crying and hugging each other. Then he told them how Satan had laughed at him and how God didn't know him. Luke I must know Jesus right now. Please pray with me. Show me how to be saved or I will surely die and go to Hell with the Devil.

Luke smiled at Diane through his tears. He knew she had prayed many prayers for her beloved father. He also knew the other pretty lady was his precious Beverly.

"It would be a pleasure sir. I'd like nothing better than to lead you to Jesus. He loves you and He's been waiting for you to invite him into your heart."

Diane had never seen her father like this. The tears running down his face told her he was sincere. She was so thankful that her sweet Jesus had somehow broken through that wall of separation. He had broken that stony heart of her father and made it new again.

"Grandmother, God just answered our prayers for Daddy." she whispered, as she looked up to the ceiling she imagined a star filled heaven.

As John knelt to pray Rebecca, J.P., Jillian, Alex, Adeline, and Diane all knelt beside him. That night the entire Cavender family gave their hearts to Jesus. He knew how he would vote now. The ship would be docking that afternoon and they would all be flying home.

As John knelt down to pray that night, he told Jesus how he had always hoped to be president. He told Jesus how sorry he was for putting that desire before Him. He asked Jesus to forgive him. He also asked God to lead him as he went to cast his vote. He knew how to vote, but before he did he had some things to say to his esteemed colleges. He also wanted to tender his resignation. He couldn't do things their way anymore. He would serve God, the way he promised Him he would. Nothing else mattered to John. He knew how real Hell was, and it was only through the goodness and mercy of God that he and his family would escape that awful place. He knew now, that God so loved the world that He gave His Son. He knew that the Bible was The Word of God and it was truth. He also knew without a doubt that Jesus had died for his sins. He knew that Jesus bore his shame and guilt on the cross. He would forevermore be thankful to God for saving his soul. Being president really didn't matter anymore. John was a new man, he had a new life, and he would live it for Jesus.

The next day when the ship docked Luke and Diane immediately left for Nashville. They wanted to contact all the churches that had taken part in fighting for Christian Freedoms to be alerted as to what God was doing for them. They had promised John they would be there for the vote.

Rebecca was real chatty on the plane ride home. She was delighted that God had saved her and her entire family. She was so thankful that Luke had spent all that time teaching them from the Bible. She thought about Sara. She had prayed for so long and God was still answering her prayers even though she had gone on to heaven years ago. Rebecca knew now what perfect peace was. It was the first time in her life that she had experienced such unconditional love. That's what Jesus had given her. She couldn't wait until they got home. She was going to find a church and start attending right away. She had so much to learn, and she was anxious to get started. John was so different, she observed. He was the picture of peace as was the rest of the family. No one could ask for more than this she thought.

As Diane and Luke rallied the Christians to march on Washington, John was busy writing his speech. They could do whatever they wanted to him, he didn't care about his career. He just wanted to serve God. It was late Sunday night when he finally finished his speech. He was due to vote right after lunch on Monday. Diane and Luke arrived very early Monday morning. The town was filling up. There was not an empty space to be found in Washington that day there were people everywhere you looked. At last the Christians would be heard. They were there to support John. He was their brother in Christ now. There is always hope in Jesus you just have to stand, and he will do the rest.

"We are standing," they said. "We will not give up our rights any longer. We have the power of almighty God on our side."

By noon there was more than twenty million Christians and more on the way.

John felt so good he wanted to shout.

"What freedom" he said. "This is what our forefathers died for." Then he whispered "Jesus this is what you died for"

The Senate was buzzing with excitement. "Today we rule." David Forman said. His voice sounded a little shrill. He had twisted a lot of arms to get this bill passed and it would be law in a few hours. When John voted and the president signed it into law, David's future would be secure. Money was the only thing that interested him and there would be a huge payoff at the end of this day. He could leave politics and live a life of luxury. Who cared about the next election? He would finish his work in this term.

President William Noble had decided to sit in on the vote. He thought he would support John. He knew John could never be president after he cast his vote. No one would vote for him.

CHAPTER THIRTY

The Vote

When John took the podium, it was deathly quiet on the Senate Floor. Most of the Conservatives looked tired and beat. Most on the other side were jubilant as they waited for John to cast his vote. As John looked around the room he could see the stress on many of their faces. They may had voted with his party but they were not happy about this at all, he thought. David Forman couldn't hide his happiness. He was sure this was the day he had been waiting for. Today he would make history. No more Christian radio or television. No more churches or Bibles. No more Preachers or Gospel Singers telling them how wrong they were, or preaching family values and morality. He was even a little glad that all the Christians had gathered for the great event. Hopefully most of them would end up in jail before the day was over.

John cleared his throat and started to speak as the doors of the chamber opened and Luke walked in with Rebecca, J.P. Jillian, Alex, Adeline and Diane. The buzz was deafening.

"What's he doing here?" they asked about Luke.

"We thought he had been stopped. And look, why is John's family with him?"

John smiled broadly as he invited his family and his dear friend Luke to join him. He said, "Honored Senators it brings me great pleasure today to cast the tiebreaking vote for you. The Liberals started cheering and gave him a two minute standing ovation. Luke couldn't help but smile. They actually thought he was there for them. That he had changed course that somehow John had persuaded him over to their side. Then the chamber's door opened again and Christians from everywhere marched in and either took a seat or stood quietly. Each one had a Bible in their hands. When no one else could enter they filled the gallery, lobbies and the streets. There were people as far as you could see in every direction. They were marching to victory. The press was in a frenzy, they loved this kind of drama. Many of them already had stories written about the end of Christianity. Dan had gotten there early. Luke had called him as soon as he got into Nashville.

John cleared his throat again. "I guess we're all here now" he said with a jovial laugh.

"My friends something wonderful happened to me on the night you all voted. I went to bed, went to sleep, and then...I went to hell."

He told them of the dream he had and how God himself had shown him what a terrible mistake it would be to go against Him. Then he told them of the scriptures his mother had often read him. Sometimes paraphrasing, and sometimes looking into the Bible his mother had left for him. She had the verses all marked. She knew someday he would need them.

"That ye that did cleave unto the Lord your God, are alive every one of you this day. I wanted life," John said, "So in the middle of the night I prayed the Sinner's Prayer. I asked Jesus to be my Savior."

Then he looked back into the scriptures. "Surely this great nation is a wise and understanding people. For what nation is there so great, who hath God so nigh unto them, as the Lord our God is in all things that we call upon him for? And what nation is there so great, that hath statues and judgments so righteous as all this law, which

I set before you this day? So we must take heed to ourselves, and keep our souls diligently, lest we forget the things which our eyes have seen, and lest they depart from our heart all the days of our life: but teach our sons and grandsons. This is what our forefathers did for us, which made us this great nation that we are today."

Now the Conservatives were standing. Tears were streaming down the faces of all who were listening. The Christians were silently praying for they knew that God was still on the throne.

"Therefore," John continued, "I cannot, and will not vote to remove Christianity from our Great Nation." I would rather be a janitor in the house of the Lord than to be president and go against my Jesus."

John thought to himself, now I sound like my mother. Then he cast his vote against the bill. It went down in defeat. All over the country people were singing "God Bless America." The streets of every small town, and big city were filled with happy voices cheering for that final vote. The Secret Service had to get John and his family to their car and out of the city. The Christians had come to support John and they meant to do just that. The signs were ready to go. And the people began chanting John for president. Similar scenes from all across the Country were all over the evening news. There was joy everywhere.

Luke turned on the news. He quickly called Diane to tell her and her family what was going on. Diane was praising the Lord for his goodness to them. She was still crying when they hung up, but they were tears of joy. John's phone didn't stop ringing the rest of the night. The Senators from both parties were trying to get him to run on their ticket. The Evangelicals were going to support him no matter what ticket he was on. That evening he opened his mother's Bible and another scripture that she had marked reached out and touched him.

"Seek ye first the kingdom of God, and his righteousness; and all these things shall be added unto you." John knew he could probably win the presidency now, because God was with him. He didn't care about that now, he cared about God and His will. Being president was no longer his top priority. John was truly free for the first time in his life. All fear was gone.

William called at nine o'clock. John was feeling very relaxed as he took the call. William was beside himself.

"I don't claim to understand this he told John, but I believe you made the right choice. You probably saved us all from disaster. I am proud of you for listening to your heart. The Liberals in the Senate have been calling all evening. Most of them were threatened into voting for the bill. They are so thankful that you killed it. They have said they will back you if you run for president I would consider it if I were you."

John assured him he would think about it. He told William he might have to change parties. "You know that more and more I believe in the conservative way. As a Christian I can no longer support abortion. I also have a big problem with the A.F.A. fighting against all our Christian beliefs. I may change as soon as your term is over. I do have to follow my heart."

As the days rolled by John became more and more popular with the voters. They knew where he stood and even the Liberals were coming on board. They believed that he had saved them all from making a huge mistake. They knew it wasn't right to ban religion. They were just listening to the big money people, but John had showed them a better way.

David Foreman left the senate with his head bowed low. Anger filled his heart. He hated John, for he had just taken from him everything he had worked for. His career was over, and he had failed. There would be no big payday now, no life of luxury. He might as well be dead. The next morning his wife found his lifeless body hanging from a rafter in their basement.

CHAPTER THIRTY ONE

In Love

It has been a year now since Beverly was killed. The people responsible have all been put away for life. Luke's church is overflowing with new members, including the vice president and his entire family. They fly into Nashville nearly every Sunday to attend church. Luke is a frequent visitor to The White House. He believes John has a good chance at being the next president of the United States if he decides to run. That is still a little up in the air. John wants to run, but he needs a good vice president, someone who agrees with his policies. He really needs a Christian partner. John prays about it daily.

Diane is very happy in Nashville. Her law practice is growing so rapidly she is considering a partner. Diane and Luke are very good friends and often share time together. Luke has brought his children home and Little Rebecca is living with Diane full time now. They both have nannies to help care for the children and they often do things together. Their families are close. She knows he is the best friend she has ever known. He feels the same way about her. Fredrick and Beverly had died so close to the same time that she and Luke have gone through the grieving process together. The pain has subsided, but not the memories. They are both ready to move on with their lives.

Diane asks Luke if he would consider taking a vacation with her, just the two of them and their children. He tells her he will pray about it and let her know. After a few days he tells her he doesn't think it would be appropriate for just the two families to vacation together. "The critics of the church would have something to talk about." He says he knows that nothing would happen but others may not believe this to be possible. Then he confesses that he isn't sure he can trust his feelings enough to be alone with her in a vacation atmosphere. She is devastated at his reaction, and tells him so.

"I would never do anything to harm your ministry and you know that, she cried. He quickly puts his arms around her and says,

"I know you wouldn't sweet Diane, but my feelings for you are growing stronger every day and sometimes I believe I am falling in love with you. Tears run down his face and Diane can feel his pain. She is so sorry she has placed him in this position.

Suddenly reality sets in and she realizes she loves him too. "Luke I want to be with you and your children. I'm falling in love with you too. I know that Fredrick and Beverly will always have a special place in our hearts. I loved Fredrick and I'd give my own life for him if I could, but I can't and life must go on. Luke I wouldn't have gotten through this past year without you. You have been my strength and my best friend. Now I believe that we need more than friendship. I love you and I don't want to be anywhere without you. Surely God put us together and I trust him to know what's best for us.

Luke just stood stunned for a few seconds and then he grabbed her and held her like he would never let go. He knew she was right. He believed that God had put them together to help each other and had given them a special love for each other.

"We will have our vacation he said but it will have to be a honeymoon." She clung to him crying and saying over and over that she loved him. He could feel the pain leaving his heart and healing taking its place. He kissed her at last and he knew it was alright. Then he remembered the last conversation he and Fredrick had before he died. Fredrick was being threatened and he feared he would be killed, so he asked Luke to take care of his family if anything happened to him. He also asked him to keep up the fight.

"Thank you my friend," Luke whispered. "I will honor your request, because I love her too. We will never stop fighting for the cause of Christ, and we will meet you in heaven."

"Diane are you serious?" Rebecca cried in a happy voice. "We must get busy on wedding plans. I am so happy for both of you. You deserve happiness." The plan was to marry the following year. They wanted to be married in Luke's church with Brian one of his pastor friends officiating the ceremony.

After church on Sunday, John and Luke sat in his study discussing politics and the Bible. "Luke, sometimes I wish I had your job. It would be wonderful to just study and preach and teach others about our wonderful Lord. I read Mother's Bible every day. I just can't get enough of it. I'm like a starving man. I feast on The Word every day and still want more. My mother loved the Bible so much, and so do I. I'm glad she left it for me. Next to my salvation it's the greatest gift anyone ever gave me. I even enjoy the little notes she wrote as she studied. I feel as though she is still here teaching me, the way she tried to do when I was a child."

Luke was amazed to hear John talking like this. He truly did love God and it showed, but Luke never knew the interest John had in the ministry.

"It would be wonderful to have you as an assistant pastor," Luke said with a big smile. "I know it wouldn't be the same as being president. It is a very thankless job at times, yet it is the most rewarding work there is. I wouldn't trade places with the president. I love to serve my God, and John I'm very proud of all the changes I have witnessed in your life. God can use a man like you as president. You can serve him in every situation. Our country needs more people like you running our government."

"Thank you son." John answered.

Both men knew their destiny. John would be president and Luke would be his son-in-law and spiritual adviser.

CHAPTER THIRTY TWO

Thinking of Running for Congress

The next year was a busy one. Luke and Diane were helping John with his campaign. He was expected to win the election. Rebecca was also campaigning with John. It seemed the whole country had embraced this lovely woman. The people responded to Rebecca. They knew she would be a wonderful first lady. Rebecca whose only desire in life was to have a family felt as though the whole country was now her family.

J.P. was thinking about getting into politics himself. He was sure his father would support his ambitions. He thought he would like to run for Congress. He wasn't thinking about being president or even vice president. After seeing his father take the stand that he did for the country, J.P. felt he too should offer his service to his country. His plans were based on the deep love for his country and the people that make it so great. He had learned that from his father. The country must have responsible leaders. We must never again entertain the idea of taking the freedoms of any group in America. We are all created equal and should treat everyone with the same respect. J. P. was very proud of his father and he wanted to follow in his footsteps. He knew he would do all he could to protect the citizens of America.

CHAPTER THIRTY THREE

Abusive Parents

Jillian was very proud of her husband. She had a wonderful family. She was so thankful that they had all made Jesus their Savior. She didn't cry all the time now. The pain of her past was being healed daily. Jillian had come from a prominent family. From the outside everything looked good, but there was much abuse in her household. She would run to her nanny for protection from her father and mother who became very abusive when they were drinking. They drank quite often, when they were at home, where no one could see them. She never spoke of the abuse to anyone except a Christian counselor she had met at church. Marie had sought her out to get involved with a children's program she was heading up. Marie was an abuse counselor. She counseled both children and adults. Jillian had confided in her and Marie had been counseling with her privately. Her life was so much better now that God was leading her. She had agreed to serve on the board of directors of several charities.

She enjoyed working to benefit abused children. She knew you didn't have to be poor to be a victim of abuse. Jillian was a good mother to Alex and Adeline. She never wanted her children to feel the way she had most of her life. Jillian was looking forward to

Diane and Luke's wedding. Diane had asked her and the children to take part in the wedding. Little Rebecca will be the flower girl. J.P. would be Best Man. They all loved Luke very much and knew he would be an asset to their family.

CHAPTER THIRTY FOUR

Visiting Beverly's Parents

It was a warm spring day in May when Luke knelt at Beverly's grave. He thanked her for being his wife. He told her about his love for their children and finally he said that he would always love her, but the time had come for him to remarry. He hoped she would understand. Luke knew this was a little crazy, but he had always confided in Beverly, and out of respect for her and their life together he wanted to do it one last time. He felt at peace now and knew he was ready to move on. Next month he would marry Diane and begin a new life with her and their children, but he would never forget Beverly. She was the first woman he had ever loved. They were very close, not only as husband and wife, but she was his best friend. When she died a part of him seemed to die with her. Diane had helped him to think that life could be good again.

Just as he started to leave, he heard Diane calling his name.

She said, "I thought I'd find you here. I have been to Fredrick's grave already. I had to tell him good-by. I know he would be very happy for us." With that said she put her arms around Luke and whispered

"I love you," and she did too. "We will be alright."

Luke loved her so much, at times like these. She always knew what to say to make him feel better.

He knew he would have to visit Beverly's mom and dad to tell them of his plans to remarry. He decided he would go this weekend. He wanted them to hear this from him and not read it in the newspaper. He and Diane had kept their plans very private. They had only shared them with her family until now.

CHAPTER THIRTY FIVE

Wedding Plans

Diane was being fitted for her wedding gown. She had let her blonde hair hang loose for the fitting. It was long and silky. Fredrick had always loved her hair. She hadn't worn it down since his death. She had worn it in a French twist. A sophisticated look for the court room and the office but not very pretty for a wedding. She planned on wearing her hair loose under her wedding veil. Luke had given her a beautiful diamond engagement ring and they had purchased matching wedding bands. She knew Luke would be going to speak with Beverly's parents. That was one more reason why she loved him so much. He cared deeply about others. She had spoken to Fredrick's father. His mother was dead. His father wished her well. He had sent a check for one thousand dollars for a wedding gift. He was a good man and she let him know that he would always be welcome in their lives. He could visit little Rebecca as often as he wished. Father Shell said he would love to meet Luke. He had heard so much about him from Fredrick. Diane asked if he would like to come to the wedding. He said he couldn't come at this time, but would plan a trip for Christmas if that was okay with everyone. She assured him he would be most welcome.

Rebecca and Jillian were overseeing all the preparations for the wedding. The church would be filled with red roses. The choir would sing the wedding songs, they had been practicing for weeks. Diane had taken a month off from work. She and Luke would leave right after the reception for their honeymoon in Paris France. A wedding gift from her parents. Diane couldn't remember the last time she had been this happy. Only God could do something this wonderful for her, and she was very thankful.

Luke left for Beverly's parent's home early Saturday morning. He knew they would be disappointed because the boys hadn't come. They were away at church camp. Mr. and Mrs. Berry welcomed Luke into their home. He was right, they sure were disappointed that the boys hadn't come this time. Mrs. Berry had made a light lunch for them.

Afterwards as they sat sipping sweet tea Luke finally got to the reason he had come. He told them how much he had loved Beverly, and would always cherish her memory. Tears filled their eyes when he told them how lonely he had been without her. Then he told them about Diane and her family and how much they had helped him and the boys to adjust. He told them about Fredrick and the promise he had made to him after Beverly was killed. Then he told them about his love for Diane and her love for him and the boys.

As he finished Mrs. Berry put her arms around him and thanked him for considering their feelings like he did. She told him to please be happy and to know they would always be there for him and the boys and there was plenty of love in them to share with Diane too. They asked if they could meet her and of course he said yes. They both hugged him as he was leaving and told him that they loved him.

Luke couldn't help but shed a few tears on his way home. The goodness of the Lord flowed through His people. No wonder Beverly was so special. Her parents had taught her to love and accept others.

Diane was waiting for Luke when he arrived home. She held him close as he told her about his visit with the Berry's. Diane asked if he would mind if she sent them a note to let them know they would always be a part of their lives. Luke said that it would be a good thing. Diane wrote the note that very night. She also told them they were welcome to come to their wedding if they would like too. If not, to plan a visit real soon. The boys would love to see them and so would she and Luke. A few days later Diane received a note from the Berry's saying they would love to come to their wedding, and also, to take the boys for the summer if it was okay.

Luke called them that evening assuring them that it was more than okay. He told them their wedding invitation should arrive in a day or two. They sounded really happy for him. Once again Luke understood why Beverly had been so wonderful. He wished he had gotten to know the Berry's better while Beverly was still alive. Their relationship had been a little awkward since her death. Maybe it's still not too late he thought. He knew Diane would love them. Maybe his new family could help fill the terrible void in their lives. Beverly had been their only child.

CHAPTER THIRTY SIX

Wedding Day

John was on the campaign trail most of the time now. Rebecca traveled with him as much as she could.

Jillian was very busy helping with the wedding arrangements and J.P. had just entered the Senate race. Right after Diane and Luke's wedding they too would be on the campaign trail. She would not be able to go as much as Rebecca when school was in session, but she could travel with him all summer. She had never seen their family so happy and fulfilled as they were right now.

Luke awoke early that June morning and smiled as he remembered what day it was. He knelt by his bed and prayed sincerely to God. He thanked him for all his many blessings and just as he did everyday he thanked him for his salvation. He told him how happy he felt to be marrying Diane today. He asked God to let him be a good husband to her and a good father to her little girl. As he ended his prayer he could hear the boys stirring around in the living room. He knew they would be hungry. All of a sudden he felt hungry too.

The boys came into Luke's bedroom and asked him what was for breakfast. They told him they had been too excited to sleep. Diane would become their mommy today, they were so happy. They loved her very much. They thought about their real mommy and knew she would be happy for them. They needed a mom and God was giving them one. The boys, Mark and Nathan would also have a little sister. They called her Becca. She was a lot of fun to play with. For Nathan it was nice not having to be the baby anymore. Now he would be a big brother too just like Mark was.

Mr. and Mrs. Berry arrived in Nashville at noon. The wedding was scheduled for six in the evening and the reception was to follow. They went to their hotel and called Luke from there. He sounded so happy. They knew this was the right thing for all of them. They were going to meet Diane for the first time today at lunch. She had invited them all to her house. They were due to arrive there at one o'clock. They were excited to see the boys and even more excited that they were going to take them home for the summer. They had all kinds of plans for their visit.

Diane had a wonderful cook and housekeeper. The table was set with their best china, silver, and crystal, and decorated with flowers of every color. The setting was breathtakingly beautiful. There were huge bowls of fruit, steaming hot soup and thick steaks, garden salad, and baked potatoes. She seated the Berrys between Mark and Nathan. She seated her mom and dad next to Becca as they were all calling her now. Jillian and J.P. sat with their children Alex and Adeline and Luke sat at the head of the table and she sat opposite him at the other end. It was a beautiful sight. Mr. and Mrs. Berry were happy to get to meet John and Rebecca at last. They assured John he would be getting their vote in November. The Cavender family were so kind and gracious to them that soon they were talking as though they had known each other for ages. Everyone was very careful not to do anything to hurt this wonderful couple whose daughter had been ripped from them. They had suffered a very great loss yet they were willing to open their hearts and lives to Diane and Becca.

After lunch Luke took the boys home with him and invited the Berry's to come home with them. They decided to go back to their hotel to rest before the wedding. Luke understood. He kissed them both on the cheek and thanked them for being there. He said for them to be at the church by 5:30 so they could be seated with the proper honors. The service would begin at six o'clock.

Diane took a leisurely bath and gathered all her things together to take to the church. She wanted to be there at four o'clock to have her hair and nails done. They would do her makeup at five and she would get dressed at five thirty. She was nervous, excited and so very happy.

Beverly's mom and dad were glad they had come. They were very impressed with Diane and her family. They knew their grandsons would be loved and cared for. They also knew that Beverly would approve. Luke was a wonderful young man and he deserved every happiness that life could afford him. They knew he had suffered terribly when their daughter was killed. He never stopped serving God and they hadn't either. They had heard about John's dream, and how happy he said Beverly was in heaven. They knew that it was just the retelling of a dream, but that dream had been such a powerful force for good that they believed it had come from God. It comforted them for now and they knew they would see her again in Heaven, and never be separated any more.

They had decided to visit her grave this afternoon before going to the church. They bought a beautiful flower arrangement on their way. They were going to place them on her headstone. As they approached her grave they saw Diane kneeling there. Their hearts filled with love for this young woman that God had sent into their lives. They stayed back and waited until Diane got up to leave. They saw that she was wiping tears from her eyes. Mrs. Berry walked over and took her in her arms. They cried together and then they wiped their tears and promised not to cry any more. They decided that it would be better to live each day in honor of Beverly and Fredrick. Mr. Berry told her he hoped she would have a happy life.

As he kissed her cheek he said, "We will be here for you any time you need us."

Diane thanked them and headed for the church to begin her new life.

Luke arrived at the church at five o'clock. He had gotten the children dressed at home and he would get dressed in his office. Their nanny was helping him with the kids. Mark and Nathan would be seating their grandparents, and Alex and Adeline would be seating their grandmother and the Berrys. Then they would seat John after he gave the bride away. The children were well practiced. The boys were wearing tuxedos and the girls were wearing white dresses made of French lace. They were quite beautiful. Luke put on his white tuxedo and J.P. was wearing a black one with a teal shirt. Jillian was stunning in her teal dress also made from French lace. She was so pretty that J.P. told her she was as beautiful as the bride. She blushed, but he could tell she was pleased.

It was exactly six o'clock when the choir started singing, "The Lord's Prayer" The chimes rang out through the huge sanctuary. They sang the "Halleluiah Praise." Luke and J.P. stepped out to the front of the church and the children lined up on either side. Next, Becca came slowly walking down the aisle dropping rose petals and Jillian walked slowly behind her. As they reached the front of the church, the giant organ began to play "The Wedding March".

Then the preacher invited everyone to stand. John and Diane made their way down the aisle. He held her arm and reassured her he wouldn't let her fall. She was the most radiant bride anyone had ever seen. Her dress was layered with lace and sparkled with diamonds. The train was very long and her hair was flowing beneath her veil. She was beautiful. Luke felt his eyes welling up and he knew that hers were too.

The ceremony was not very long, even though they pledged their love to each other and then each promised the children they were marrying them too. Becca was so pretty in her little white dress as Luke slipped a little diamond ring on her finger and kissed her.

She said, "Thank you my Daddy."

By then tears were flowing all over the church. Diane put her arms around Mark and Nathan and promised she would never try to take their mother's place. She said that she would be the best mother she knew how to be, and she would always love them. Next it was time for the children to embrace each other and Becca couldn't hug her brothers tight enough.

Soon they were all married and a new family had begun. The Berrys felt as if they had a new daughter and they promised God they would love her as their own. It was decided that they would be called Mom and Dad Berry and they would be invited to all family get-togethers from now on. All in all it was a perfect wedding.

They were announced for the first time as The New Davis Family. As they walked into the reception hall the music was already playing. Luke took his bride in his arms and they danced to "The Wedding Song." The boys each danced with Becca and then their new mom as Becca stole the show by dancing with her feet on top of her new Daddy's shoes. It was the official beginning of their new lives together and it was a joyous occasion.

It seemed to come to an end way too soon. The bride and groom had to excuse themselves so they could go get dressed. They had a plane to catch at eleven o'clock. The limousine was already there to take them to the airport. J.P. and Jillian would play host and hostess for the rest of the evening. John and Rebecca invited the Berrys to come for a visit real soon. The Berrys accepted their invitation. They would be calling them to schedule it as soon as they got back from their honeymoon. John promised he would give them a tour of the White House. He even said, if he won the election he would invite them there for a weekend and they could stay in the Lincoln Bedroom.

They assured him that he would win and they would come to visit. Mr. Berry asked John if they could help with his campaign. John said he would welcome their help. The Berrys said they would help him win the state of Tennessee. Before they left they gave him a generous donation for his campaign and promised they would get to work right away.

CHAPTER THIRTY SEVEN

President John Paul Cavender

The next two weeks, while Luke and Diane were on their honeymoon, the kids were vacationing with their grandparents. Becca had begged to go with her brothers and the Berrys had taken her home with them too. They had a great time, all of them. Dad Berry was busy lining up places for John to speak all over the state of Tennessee. He had thousands of friends and they were getting out the vote. What a great time he was having. He hadn't felt this good in years. John and Rebecca were looking forward to the trip to Tennessee. The Berrys insisted they stay at their house.

"It's not as fancy as the White house," they said, "But you will have all the comforts of home." John and Rebecca looked forward to having some time with these good people. They were not disappointed either. The speaking engagements were drawing thousands of people and Thomas and Mary, as the Berrys finally asked to be called, were on every radio and TV station in Tennessee getting out the vote. Tennessee, being a religious state, already knew who John was, and they were excited to help get him elected.

By the time the newlyweds got back from honeymooning the families were old friends. John was way ahead in the polls. The country was behind him all the way. The evangelicals were also on every station in the nation reminding their fellow Christians that John needed their help now. He came to their aid and now they must help him. They sent donations of every size to his headquarters, and put up signs everywhere they could be put. John was so humbled by the goodness of God's people he sometimes just broke down and cried. Whether he was elected president or not, this was the most wonderful time of his life. He was rejoicing in the Lord always. His mother had taught him that expression years ago and now he knew what it meant.

Finally election-day arrived. The polls opened at six o'clock in Nashville and Thomas and Mary were the first to vote in their precinct. The turnout was record breaking all over the country. John was busy visiting as many places as he could. Finally he gathered his family together to wait for the results in their hotel suite near his Campaign Headquarters. Of course the Berrys had flown up with Luke, Diane and the children to wait with them. As they waited they prayed for God to do His perfect will. Around seven thirty the early predictions started coming in. John was running ahead in the East. Next he was running ahead in the heart of the country and finally he was way ahead out West. By ten o'clock it was a sure thing. John had won by a landslide. He was now The President Elect of the United States of America. As he headed for his campaign headquarters he prayed all the way for God to be in everything he said or did. He gave the job over to Jesus and promised he would do things His way.

"All my life," He said, "I wanted to be president, and God has given me this honor. Now I want to honor Him, and all of you, in all I do." As John spoke to his supporters he told them all how this was made possible by a man named Jesus. "This country was founded on His Word and as long as I'm president he will be honored again in this country, as he deserves to be."

John told his people that there would be many hard times ahead. "Satan will never stop fighting God's people. He hates the church and will defile it in any way he can. We must always be on guard to protect The Word of God and the Church that belongs to Him. God has proven Himself over and over and He will always defeat evil. I am president today because God willed it. He makes no mistakes and He loves us unconditionally. To God be the glory forever. Amen."

The End

ABOUT THE AUTHORS

Margie J. Pittman and Barbara Reed are a mother and daughter tandem. Barbara was born in Cleveland, Ohio, and has spent most of her life in the Charleston, West Virginia, area. Margie, a Charleston native, is well-known for her Coal Camp Kids trilogy chronicling her upbringing in a Campbell's Creek, West Virginia, coal camp. Knowing her mother's love for writing, Barbara called one day and said she had a book idea. Margie loved the personal, political, and Christian struggle that were woven throughout Barbara's story outline. The resulting story from their collaboration is plausible, maybe even probable, based on current trends in America. They hope you enjoy Tiebreaker and ask that you pray for our country.

Printed in the United States
By Bookmasters